THEY STAND—
SIX-GUNS IN HAND!

WILL CARSTON: The U.S. Marshal lets his sons learn some lessons the hard way—until the law gets shattered in Twin Rifles . . .

WASH CARSTON: The former Rebel has always had ideas of his own. This time they're leading him straight into a fight . . .

CHANCE CARSTON: He lives by his fists and his wits. When the former Union soldier gets wronged, someone is sure to pay . . .

PHINEAS McDOUGAL: He came to town with plans to start a bank. But behind the plan is a far more brutal deal . . .

JOHN FITCH: The local farmer trusted McDougal with his money. His second mistake was trying to stand up to a murderous band of outlaws . . .

WALTER LAWRENCE: All of a sudden the long-time Twin Rifles banker had some competition in town. What he didn't know was how much he stood to lose . . .

Books by Jim Miller

Ranger's Revenge
The Long Rope
Hell with the Hide Off
Too Many Drifters

Published by POCKET BOOKS

Most Pocket Books are available at special quantity discounts for bulk purchases for sales promotions, premiums or fund raising. Special books or book excerpts can also be created to fit specific needs.

For details write the office of the Vice President of Special Markets, Pocket Books, 1230 Avenue of the Americas, New York, New York 10020.

TOO MANY DRIFTERS

JIM MILLER

POCKET BOOKS
New York   London   Toronto   Sydney   Tokyo   Singapore

This book is a work of fiction. Names, characters, places and incidents are either the product of the author's imagination or are used fictitiously. Any resemblance to actual events or locales or persons, living or dead, is entirely coincidental.

An *Original* Publication of POCKET BOOKS

POCKET BOOKS, a division of Simon & Schuster Inc.
1230 Avenue of the Americas, New York, NY 10020

Copyright © 1991 by James L. Collins

All rights reserved, including the right to reproduce
this book or portions thereof in any form whatsoever.
For information address Pocket Books, 1230 Avenue
of the Americas, New York, NY 10020

ISBN: 0-671-73271-4

First Pocket Books printing July 1991

10 9 8 7 6 5 4 3 2 1

POCKET and colophon are registered trademarks of
Simon & Schuster Inc.

Cover art by Gavin Baker

Printed in the U.S.A.

*With a great deal of respect
and admiration for my brothers,
Mark and Jeff, and their lovely wives,
Gretchen and Sue, respectively.*

TOO MANY DRIFTERS

CHAPTER
★ 1 ★

It turned out to be one hell of a day. And it all started even before the sun arose. I was in the kitchen area of the ranch house, trying to remember the recipe Sarah Ann had given me for making flapjacks. Actually, it wasn't the making of flapjacks I was trying to perfect. It was mixing up enough flour and water and whatever to make the mix come out good enough so my brother Chance wouldn't complain about them. I took a sip of coffee, which I'd gotten fairly good at brewing, and scratched the back of my head, trying to conjure up the missing ingredients Sarah Ann had mentioned to me more than once. I was asking myself an age-old question—why is it women come so easy to cooking while men can't do it worth spit?—when I heard a thud outside.

The sun was just making its orange appearance on the eastern horizon when I pulled back the makeshift curtain and glanced out the window to see Chance getting up off the ground in the corral. Even in that little light I could tell my brother was off to a bad start. Of course, all it took was seeing Nightmare prancing around across the corral to know it was going to be another bad day for Chance.

"Need a hand?" I yelled out, knowing that the words were as useless as buffalo chips in a fancy back-East salad. Chance had been fighting that wild mustang for the better part of a week now, determined to ride him or die. So far all he'd done was collect dust on the bottom of his britches and make a big deal of brushing it off when what he really had was not only a dusty bottom but a sore one to boot.

"Hell no, little brother," he growled without looking at me. "I'm gonna break this sonofa—"

"Hotcakes coming up soon, Chance," I interrupted. Chance threw me a glare I gauged to be as dangerous as the one he'd just finished giving Nightmare, the mustang he aimed to conquer come hell or high water. Just between you and me, I figured Texas would be free of drought before my brother ever tamed the horse out in that corral. But then the horse business was what we were trying to get into, so I reckon you couldn't blame Chance for being as determined as he was. Of course, Pa has been calling that particular trait of my brother's bullheadedness for years.

"I'll take some coffee and hold off on them flapjacks until you show me you can make 'em proper," Chance said, dusting his hat off against his pants and tossing it toward a peg on the wall he'd become proficient at hitting. "What you rustled up yesterday left one helluva lot to be desired." That was Chance, always griping about something.

When I remembered it was baking soda that was missing from my recipe, Chance had gone through a second cup of coffee and positioned himself in the doorway, staring at Nightmare as though the horse was the only thing on this earth worth looking at. Saying that he was obsessed with breaking that mustang would have described the look on his face only mildly. The man I was looking at had a bit of madness to him, the kind I suspected my brother had fancied during his days in the Union cavalry. The War Between the States had been over about a year and a half now, but guys like Chance and me who had been in it still carried many memories.

"Not bad," he said later, pushing his plate away. "I might just take you in one day and ask Big John Porter if he'd be willing to take you on as a cook."

"Not on your life," I said and poured us both the remains of the coffee. Big John Porter was Sarah Ann's father. He was also owner and proprietor of the Porter Cafe in Twin Rifles. And if you're wondering, Big John lived up to his name. Both Chance and I topped six foot easy, but Sarah Ann's daddy had a good six or eight inches on each of us. No sir, you'd best stay away from Big John.

It was an hour into sunup when Chance threw out the rest of his coffee and decided he was burning daylight. Before he left to go back to Nightmare and the one-man feud he was waging with the animal, I told him I'd be heading into Twin Rifles for some more flour later in the morning.

"Some day you're gonna do some goddamn work around here, Wash," he grumbled as I started to walk off.

"I do work." I smiled at him.

"Like hell."

I shrugged. "I can't help it if you decided it was old Nightmare you wanted to wage a hating war with."

Then I saddled up and headed for town.

Twin Rifles was one of those small towns that stay relatively unknown to most people. Maybe it's because you can ride through it in a matter of minutes. Or maybe it's because the folks will make you feel welcome those few minutes you happen to be in town. For the most part they're gentle people who like to get on with their lives but seldom turn away a man needing help.

Will Carston was the founder of Twin Rifles. It was him and Asa Ferris who staked a claim to the place with nothing more than their Bowie knives and a rifle apiece. Hence, the name Twin Rifles. But that was before my time. Will Carston, by the way, is also the town marshal—and my pa.

I was looking at how much things had changed since I'd come back from serving the Confederacy. Or was I the one who had changed? Sometimes it was hard to tell. Most times when questions like that came up I tried to put them aside, promising myself I'd ponder them some other time, when I had time. If you know what I mean.

I stopped in at the bank and withdrew some money to buy the flour and a few other items I figured we'd be needing in the future, making a mental note that what money Chance and I had in the account probably wouldn't last until the end of the year. It being fall, that meant the end of the year wasn't far away. My next stop was the general store, where I winced as I paid for the flour, even after hearing the price being charged for it. When I left, I had a small box that carried my goods, not to mention a beleaguering thought that I had just been cheated.

I heard the ruckus in the saloon as I was about to cross in front of the batwing doors. I reckon I should have known better, but it happened anyway. The doors came flying open and the next thing I knew I was sprawled out on the dusty street, feeling like Chance must have every time that horse threw him. The items in my small box had gone scattering here and there, but what I noticed first was the sack of flour, which had broken open and was now strewn about the dust and horse apples. Beside me was the man who'd crashed into me. At first I didn't recognize him, but once he began to mumble in German, then speak in broken English, I knew it was John Fitch.

"By Got, I von't take dat no more!" he said in an angry voice as he got to his feet. "No more, no siree!" You'd have thought he was pounding his chest, his words had that much finality to them.

It was when I looked past John and the man he was directing his attention to that I got worried. Mind you, John wasn't all that big. Me, I'm kind of tall and lean, likely dwarfing the German by a good five inches or so. John Fitch, well, he was built like a pot-bellied stove, although to see him work—and I had seen him do plenty of work—you'd never guess he had so much as an ounce of fat to him. I reckon if he had anything going for him it was his bullheadedness, which immediately reminded me of Chance.

Pardee Taylor, who apparently had thrown John Fitch out of the saloon, was a whole 'nother canyon. He was tall and thick in the chest, with fists the size of my brother's. The trouble with Pardee was he didn't like anyone and he didn't care who knew it. It was also highly doubtful that he'd ever be approached by a woman to discuss the subject of matrimony. If you know what I mean. But all I needed was one glance at Pardee to know that John Fitch was no match for him and he knew it. Hell, John probably knew it too, but he had a determined look about him now and I knew that he was going to try to take him. Pride and all that, you know.

I scrambled to my feet as fast as I could, trying to think of some way to stop this fracas, knowing in the back of my mind that I'd walked into the middle of it, like it or not. Ma always said I could charm the birds from the trees, but I never have been able to figure out what she was talking about. The answer to that dilemma didn't come to me any easier as I stepped between the two men, both of them closing on one another.

"Howdy, John," I said with a smile, then quickly turned to Pardee Taylor, the look on my face changing completely. Hell, I never did like him. "Pardee, I hope you brought a good deal of cash to town with you today."

"Not hardly." He sounded as belligerent as he looked. "I'm just trying to get rid of this damned furriner." There was hate in his eyes as he gazed past me at John Fitch.

"Pardee, did you know that down south they're selling a barrel of flour for upwards of two hundred and seventy-five dollars?" I said in an even tone.

"What's that got to do with—"

"What it's got to do with anything," I interrupted, "is that I've got a strong suspicion that the folks selling flour to our general store ain't letting greed or free enterprise get in the way of competitive prices. No sir. Why, I just bought that sack of flour"—I pointed to the sack of scattered flour off to the side—"and felt like I'd had a gun stuck in my ribs for the money they took."

"Oh," Pardee said, a sly grin coming to his face now as a new realization came to him, "and you think I'm gonna pay you for that damn sack of flour? Why, you're crazy, Carston."

I turned to John Fitch and, with a straight face, said, "You know, John, he's catching on quicker than I figured him to do." But the immigrant wasn't having any funning today. He was still madder than hell, and it showed.

"You just step out of da way, Wash Carston. I take care of Mr. High and Mighty." I was beginning to wonder if I shouldn't fear John Fitch more than Pardee Taylor, if the look on his face was any indication.

Then the big man's eyes opened wide and I saw something in them that shouldn't have been there. Whether he knew it or not, it was a warning of sorts, and I'd been in too many skirmishes during the war not to notice a warning when it was coming. All I knew was that Pardee Taylor was behind me, and he was the only one I could expect any real trouble from now.

I squatted down as though some damned Yankee was taking after me and felt myself being knocked sideways as Pardee Taylor knocked my hat off, and I found myself sprawled on my side on the street again. This whole situation was getting out of hand! Why, the next thing you knew, these birds would be shooting at me with real live bullets, and I didn't want any part of that!

Pardee didn't stop at trying to hit me. He just kept on coming, heading straight for John Fitch, his original target. I kicked a foot out and threw him off balance as John Fitch stepped forward and gave Pardee one hell of a wallop across the face. He might not have been as big as Pardee, but he had big thick hands that were calloused from working the fields, and I knew the man he hit had felt it. Pardee reeled backward, stopping only when he hit the water trough next to his horse.

I was scrambling to my feet again, trying to take in the situation, when I saw that look in his eyes and knew that Pardee was about ready to go for his gun. I remembered meeting some boys in the war who'd been to places like England. They'd picked up all sorts of fancy words and sayings and such, and I'd tried to make the best of them, although at times I got them mixed up with some of my own upbringing. What came to mind now was a saying one fellow had thrown out about how it didn't matter whether you won or lost but how you played the game. Well, that may be so with those fanciful people in England, but out here, well, I'd found out that it matters not whether you win or lose *until you lose.* And Pardee Taylor didn't like to lose.

"What's going on here?" I heard Pa's agitated voice and saw him making his way across the street. All us Carstons run tall in the family tree, and Pa was no exception. He had iron-gray hair and a matching mustache. A deputy U.S. marshal's badge was pinned to his blue work shirt, and he walked with what he called a hitch in his gitalong, meaning he'd been shot in the leg back in his war, the Mexican War. He used a gnarled old hickory cane to get along, but I'd seen him do fine without it more than once. "Are you in some kind of trouble again?" he growled at me with a frown. For getting near thirty, I had the notion at times that Pa treated me like I was still a five-year-old.

"No, Mr. Marshal," John said, quickly coming to my defense. "Your Wash, he is doing fine." Then the furrow in his forehead grew deeper as he turned his attention to Pardee Taylor. "It is this one who causes the trouble, and I did nothing to start it."

"Wouldn't doubt it for a minute, Mr. Fitch," Pa said as he took in the sight of Pardee. "Taylor there, why, he ain't liked nothing since his momma let him look into a mirror. Ugly as sin and stayed that way." Pardee Taylor tightened his grip on his pistol at the sound of Pa's words, but Pa didn't miss a trick. "You know, Pardee," he added, addressing the man now in a more serious tone, "things would be a whole lot more healthful ary you was to leave that pistol where it is."

"What are you gonna do, take it from me?" he

asked in what had to be a mixture of pure hate and defiance.

"He'll do more than that, Pardee," I said. "Guaranteed."

Pa took a few more steps closer to Pardee and said, "It's like this, son. I don't want no gunplay in town, you know that. Now, ary you two fellas got a difficulty to take care of, why, I ain't got nothing against a good fistfight. No sir. It's just that now that you're in the city limits, you'll have to fight by the rules."

"Rules?" The way he said it you'd have thought Pardee Taylor had never heard of a rule in his life, and maybe he hadn't.

"Why sure. You've got to fight fair," Pa said, which turned out to be another statement Pardee had likely never heard of.

"What kind of rules?" the big bully said, a look of worry now on his face.

Pa looked at me and smiled, and when he did I knew he had the man where he wanted him. I was also reasonably sure I knew what would take place next.

"Well, for instance, there's no jabbing," Pa said, and he immediately rammed his old hickory cane into Pardee's belly button. "Like this." It took the man thoroughly by surprise, and his eyes bulged out and a gust of wind forced itself from his body. "Now, Pardee, this is a *friendly* fight, so you've got to be careful where you hit a man in the head. Might hurt him, you know, like this." That gnarled old cane came straight across the top of Pardee's forehead, and the eyes were suddenly no longer bulging but closing as he fell to the ground.

John Fitch was as surprised as some other residents

of town who had gathered once they saw Pa advancing toward us from across the street. But now that Pardee Taylor was taken care of, Pa was again turning his wrath on me.

"You know, son, I ain't gonna be around to bail you out of these scrapes forever," he growled as though it was all my fault. "You're gonna have to learn to stay out of trouble." Then he reached down and dug out a twenty-dollar gold piece from Pardee's pocket and plunked it down in my hand. "But you're right about one thing: That flour is awful goddamn high priced."

Then, without another word, he was gone.

Like I said, it was one hell of a day. But it wasn't even half through yet.

CHAPTER
★ 2 ★

John Fitch gave a tug at a chain in his pocket, pulling out his watch with thick, well-worn fingers. Once he'd given it a quick glance, he turned to me and smiled. "Come, my friend, I'll buy you a beer." Ernie Johnson, the proprietor of the saloon, was standing on the boardwalk, having taken in the fracas between Pardee Taylor and John Fitch. "If," John added, raising an eyebrow and giving Ernie a serious look, "I'm still welcome."

"Oh, sure, Mr. Fitch," the saloon man said, almost embarrassed that he had to say it, I thought. "You're welcome here any time. Any time." Ernie was basically a good man; it was just that he was slow to take sides at times. Not that there was anything bad about that, you understand, for many times it was better to pull your freight than pull your gun in this land. After all, no matter how tough a man talks, it's always better to be able to tell everyone what happened instead of laying there flat on your back and wonder how in the hell you got into this mess in the first place. Pa said that Shakespeare made comment on that somewhere along the line.

"How'd your harvesting go, John?" I asked once we'd taken a seat and the beers had arrived. I could only recall hearing this man referred to as Hans (which was his real name) by one person, and that was his wife, Greta. John Fitch was somewhere around forty-five that I could figure. I'd never had the urge to ask him outright. What I did know about him was that being a full-fledged American was one of his goals in life. I reckon that was why he'd changed from being called Hans to being called John, which I took to be the English translation of Hans. I don't know German worth spit, so I take John's explanations of which words mean which to be as honest as can be. He's that kind of man.

"Oh, nothing but trouble, mien Herr," he said in disgust and swallowed what looked to be about half his glass of beer. The first time I'd seen him do that, I'd made a mental note not to ever try to get into a drinking contest with this man. I'd have as good a set of odds of beating John Fitch at drinking as Bowie did of surviving the Alamo.

"Didn't get the crop in?"

"Oh, the crop, she come in all right," he said with a

look of surprise, "but you know, George Washington, my friend, I'm the only one working it out there, and that's a lot of work."

"Hell, John, why didn't you come get Chance and me?" I said. "We'd have gotten it done for you in no time flat."

"Yeah, I know, but I seen you boys with those horses and, how do you say? Breaking horses?"

"Yeah."

"Yeah. Vell, breaking horses is some hard work too, by golly!" His words had a good deal of force, but they held a lot of truth too. Chance and I had been trying to make a go of it in the horse business ever since we'd come back from the war, and I couldn't agree with John more. It was damn hard work. I knew from experience, for Chance wasn't the only one who'd been thrown from the top of a wild mustang.

I took a sip of the beer and looked over the rim of the glass as John ordered himself another. "You know, John, Pa would get downright offended if you told him something like that."

"This I can't help," he said with a shrug. "In the old country, a man is responsible for his own work and that is that."

"Well, there ain't nothing wrong with that at all, John," I said. "Not a thing. But you ain't in the old country now, and out here when a body gets in a bind, why, it ain't a shame to ask a neighbor for a mite of help. This is a hard land, you know, and there ain't many people who make it on their own. We all got to work together to stay alive."

John considered my words a moment, then looked at me with a smile. "Yeah, I like that, Wash. Dat is good." I was hoping he'd found another aspect of this land we called a frontier to like, for, since I'd known him—which couldn't have been more than a year—he had always been a pleasant sort of fellow. In fact, this morning was the first time I'd ever seen him get really mad.

There is something about Texas that has drawn the German population of Europe. I don't know what it is, but they've made parts of Texas their home. Maybe it's the same thing that draws those Norwegians and Swedes to the likes of Wisconsin and Minnesota. Or maybe it's finding a place to call home and then getting the word out that anyone homesick for those carrying your type of heritage can come on down to visit. Whatever it was we'd had Germans in Texas since before the Texas War for Independence. They'd dribbled in kind of slow, but they'd come. Mostly they stayed around their own, feeling more comfortable living that way, I reckon, but not John Fitch. American was what he'd wanted to be known as and he'd settled here in the Twin Rifles area back in 1863, when Chance and I were off to war. I never did know what he did in the "old country," as he called it, but farming was what he'd taken up here. He'd gotten pretty good at it too, from what I'd understood, managing to support a wife and two children through his efforts. But if things were as bad as he was claiming, well, it brought to mind my recent visit to the bank and the all too down-to-earth realization that John Fitch might soon be in the same financial straights as Chance and me were. And him with a couple of children to take care of too.

I decided it was time to show John Fitch just how

we helped out one another in this land. But I knew I was risking getting shot with the words I was about to say, for pride goes a long way, even out here, and more than one man has died of having too much of it at the wrong time.

"Say, John," I said, taking another sip of my beer and feeling almighty cautious as I continued, "if things are getting kind of tight for you and the family, I think Chance and me might be able to help you out some. If you know what I mean. Hell," I added with a shrug, "we're both single, and Chance says he's gonna be selling some of those horses right soon."

A clouded look came over John's face, and I had the spooky feeling that I was going to experience how mad this man could get again. I'd seen the way he'd taken a poke at Pardee Taylor after I had it in mind he wouldn't last worth a whit with the man, and I sure didn't want him doing the same thing to me. Then the look on his face eased a good deal and I knew I was safe—at least for the minute.

"If I had heard that from anyone else, Wash, I would have considered it an insult," he said in a whisper of a voice.

"I was just trying to—"

"I know, my friend," he replied with an understanding nod, "and believe me, I appreciate it. But no matter how good your hospitality is in this land, I must still take care of my own problems, especially where money is concerned."

I wasn't sure whether to be embarrassed or feel like a fool, but whatever it was that conjured up inside me was all sorts of confused. The best thing I could do, I thought, was keep my mouth shut.

Too Many Drifters

"A man must take care of his own, Wash," John said. "Helping a man out with his crops is one thing, for it is a favor that can be returned. But when you begin lending money to a man, he somehow becomes less of a man. I have seen many a friendship torn apart this way. And believe me, Wash, I wouldn't want us to wind up that way."

"I understand," I said, feeling godawful foolish for what I'd done.

John finished his drink and stood up to leave. He positioned his hat on his head, then gave me a solemn look and said, "A man must take care of his own, or he isn't a man."

Watching him leave, I thought I'd made a fool of myself and lost a friend, all in the space of an hour.

CHAPTER

Finances never were my long suit. I reckon that's because I've never really had all that much money. For that matter, neither did my brother. Oh, Chance was good with numbers all right, but it wasn't money he'd ever taken to counting. With Chance it was more the line of gunpowder and guns in general that held his expertise. Why, Chance could tell you right down to the last smidgen how many grains of black powder were needed for a proper load to his Colt's .44s or my old Colt's revolving shotgun or even Pa's Remington. Or do you chalk that off to nothing more than a good memory? I never was sure. Whichever it is, Chance is good when it comes to guns. Me, I got confused about buying a sack of flour in the general store. All I knew for sure was that they were charging way too much for it!

Of course, I wasn't the only one who felt that way about the economical side of life. Hell, there was too much to do in life to worry about bean counting. The closest I'd ever gotten to bean counting was that time back during the war when we were eating next to nothing and the lot of us were down to nothing but half a pot of beans and wondering how we were all going to divvy them up. But as Pa would say, that's a whole 'nother canyon.

Actually, banking has always been kind of scarce in Texas, that I recall. Before the war there weren't any federal banks in our state at all. Most of the ones we did have were privately owned and run by pretty decent people. The farmer took a loan out on what money he needed for the season in the spring and paid back what he was able to in the fall, after the crops were in and he'd made a profit. But it was the banks that made the profits, no doubt about it. Still and all, banks were always the safest place to keep your money. That is, until lately. There was that story in the papers about the fellows back in Ohio who robbed a bank. It got a lot of us to thinking that there wasn't enough jobs for some of the boys who returned from the war, but the older folks, like Pa, held a firm belief that it was the bad ones in the army who were taking to bank robbing. According to Pa, if jobs had anything to do with it, those varmints were just too damn lazy to get an honest one, and that was that!

I shook my head again as I walked out of the general store, my newly purchased sack of flour in hand. I determined that I was going to have to give up making flapjacks as often as I did, even if Chance did hold them as one of his favorite meals.

I was heading for my horse when I saw a handful of people cross the street, heading for what appeared to be some kind of rally. Or was it a fight? I wouldn't have been surprised if Pardee Taylor had come to by now and started picking fights again—he was that kind of man. I remembered Pa saying that people are curious animals, and as soon as I heard the words I found myself being drawn to them, much like the rest of the crowd, I suspected.

"And that's not all, ladies and gentlemen," a man dressed in a fancy business suit was saying to the gathering before him. He was cleanshaven and past middle age if his graying hair was any indication. Only a shade taller than medium height, I noticed he had the beginnings of a belly, a sign that he was used to good food and easy living. I couldn't see his hands that well, but I was betting they lacked calluses. His eyes appeared to jump about the crowd, as though searching out the right person for what he had in mind. All the while, his mouth was working its spiel, one I gauged he'd told a hundred times before. Being a mite taller than most folks, you get to see things that others don't, and it was right then I spotted what he had sitting next to his feet.

"Goddamn carpetbagger," Pa said, speaking my own thoughts as I spied the all-too-familiar look of the piece of baggage these type of characters were known to carry.

I couldn't tell you about the rest of the country, but down in Texas *carpetbagger* was an ugly word. As I recall, the word was first applied to so-called adventurous bankers who happened to roam west of the Mississippi to do their business and usually started their banks with the money they had, which they carried in a carpetbag. They lived out of that carpetbag the same way a drifter lives out of a bedroll. And to hear Pa talk, these types usually kept most of their proceeds in that carpetbag because if their bank failed, why, the carpetbag was the first thing they'd pick up as they headed for their horse. *Carpetbagger* had been a dirty word even before the war, but now that it was over and the Union was feeling its power, why, we called anyone from the North a carpetbagger, usually with the sure knowledge that the only reason they'd come down into our territory was to see what they could make off us in one form or another. You'd have thought that a memory like that would stick in a body's mind when pilgrims like these came around, but not this crowd. Of course, the fellow was talking about money, and that usually makes all the difference in the world on whether you get a man's attention or not. Unless you're sticking a gun in his face. That's an attention getter for sure.

"What piece of sagebrush did he come in on?" I found myself asking Pa.

"I hear he come in from the North."

"His type usually do," I said in a level tone. I had a sharp eye on the man but found myself a bit mesmerized by his words. Or maybe it was the promises he was making.

"Yes, ladies and gentlemen," he was saying, waving an enthusiastic arm in front of the crowd. It's purely amazing how diverting these fellows can be. "The Surety Savings and Loan Bank will offer you a whopping *eight percent interest* on your savings account." A stir went up in the crowd and I couldn't blame them. The Twin Rifles Bank and Trust was the only bank in town, and everyone knew the going rate of interest on a savings account was all of three percent. You'd have to have a hell of a lot of money to be able to save an awful lot, and most folks out here didn't have that much money to their name, so what this man was offering must have seemed like a minor miracle to the folks of Twin Rifles.

"Yeah, but vat do you charge on a loan?" John Fitch yelled out. "Fifteen or twenty percent?"

"No sir." The pitchman smiled back at him. "Three percent is all." Another murmur went up in the crowd. When the crowd settled down, he added, "And if you're wondering how we make a profit, we do it on sheer volume. Good people like you have the faith to invest in us and we make sure that your money is safe and ready for your withdrawal any time you need it or ask for it. And I'm sure you won't find any faults with our management, for I'm the manager of Surety."

"What'd you say your name was again?" I asked.

"McDougal. Phineas McDougal, my good man," he said with a reassuring smile.

While the man talked on and on, Pa told me how the carpetbagger had come to town early in the morning and did some checking on the available lot space in town. Before he knew it, Pa said the man had purchased the old deserted Epply building. Paid for it with cash, he did. As structures went it held up pretty good, and before long this McDougal character had hired a couple of men who claimed to be good with a hammer and nail. It was the Epply place he was standing in front of now, the hammering still going on inside.

"I wonder which army he come out of?" Pa asked as the man continued to talk.

"Wouldn't matter, Pa," was my reply. "I got a notion this one never got used to doing more than thinking." If he had an accent, I'd likely have called him a scalawag, which was just as degrading a term down south as carpetbagger. A scalawag wasn't much different, in fact. He was one of those fellows who lived in the South but didn't really support it, being for the Union cause deep down in his heart. I reckon that was about as close as you could get to being a traitor. Hell, it wasn't much more than a secret way of going over to the other side. But Phineas McDougal didn't have an accent that I could tell, so I'd just keep him in my mind as the carpetbagger I knew him to be.

"In fact," he concluded, reaching down into a vest pocket and fishing around until he came up with a pocket watch and gave it a glance, "Surety Savings and Loan will be opening at two this afternoon for new customers. I hope to see you then."

The crowd dispersed then, more than one of them heading for the Twin Rifles Bank and Trust, as Phineas McDougal stepped back inside the Epply building. Pa and I followed him into the new bank, which is about what it looked like inside. The carpenters had been hard at work, most of their hammering going into the building of a row of teller cages that they now appeared to be attaching to the walls. None of it had been painted yet, but the whole structure looked like it would do for the time being.

"You come prepared, didn't you, friend?" I said,

noting the standard iron teller cages. He had to bring those with him, for no one could put those together in that little a time. But by the looks of the place he was indeed prepared to do business. Everything was in place, ready to go.

"Tell me something, Mr. McDougal, ain't you supposed to have some kind of papers to open a bank?" Pa asked. "This sort of proceeding seems like too much responsibility to be one man's operation."

"Indeed it is," McDougal said with that same confident smile he'd had outside. "If you'll join me at my desk, I'll show you what you're looking for."

We walked around the teller cages, through a swinging gate that still needed to get used to being hinged, and back to a large desk surrounded by several boxes, some empty, some still loaded full. Full of what I couldn't tell you, nor did I care. The new banker pulled out a desk drawer and produced some papers, which he handed to Pa. Pa had been a deputy U.S. marshal for almost a year now and had done a heap of reading on the laws of the land, especially the federal ones. I remembered him telling me he didn't think there could be that many crimes to arrest a man for, so I knew he'd be well versed in defining whatever laws this man might be breaking. But he looked over the papers in his hand and gave them back to McDougal.

"I reckon it'll do for now," he said and turned to leave. Then he stopped and looked the banker square in the face. "Say, how'd you spell that name of yours?"

Phineas McDougal gave Pa a strange look and spelled out his name. "Why do you ask that, sir?"

"Oh, I just want to have the spelling right," Pa said. "You know, just in case."

"Just in case?" the man asked in a perplexed tone.

"Why, sure. Just in case you try cheating the people in this town of every red cent they have. Spelling your name right on the grave marker may be the only thing they feel like doing for you then."

Walking out the door of the bank, I thought I saw Phineas McDougal looking around desperately for a glass of water. Or a good stiff drink.

CHAPTER
★ 4 ★

"Can you beat that?" Walter Lawrence said in frustration. Seeing the tall man waiting outside Pa's office reassured my temporary doubts that all carpetbaggers looked the same. Walter Lawrence was tending toward a belly too, but he was tall, over two hundred pounds I gauged, and didn't seem like the kind of man who would take to being pushed around. But there he was in front of the marshal's office, looking like he'd been kicked in his elsewheres and told to skedaddle or he'd get kicked in the tail too. He was graying on top, likely close to the same age as Phineas McDougal. Usually he was pretty easy to get along with, but when he got mad or sad, why, his face turned into a look that you could only hang on a hound dog that won't hunt. He was sporting that look now.

"I'll bite, Walter," Pa said as we approached the door to his office. "What is it you're talking about that makes you look like you've lost your best friend?" Like most bankers, Walter Lawrence's best friend was his money, but I wasn't going to say anything to him about it. Like I said, the Twin Rifles Bank and Trust was the only bank in town.

"Why, the bank of course!" the man said, all but blowing up as he spoke. "Look! Look what they're doing to me!" Pa's hand was going down for his Remington about the same time the banker's arm shot out in the direction of the bank. I'd have had my hand on my LeMat, but I had that damn sack of flour I was still carrying. As for Pa, he only got that pistol of his out of his holster part way before setting it back in place. What he thought was going on wasn't. At least not in the manner he was thinking, which was the same as my line of thought.

"Looks like you've got a whole bunch of customers, Walter," Pa said as calm as could be. "How's business?"

"Business is lousy!" the man said, each outburst getting louder than the one before it. "Damn it, Will, do something!"

"Taking money from your bank instead of putting it in, are they?"

"Yes, Will, that's exactly what's taking place."

"Sounds like they're wanting to try out this new Phineas McDougal and his bank," I said, knowing it was likely what was on Pa's mind too.

"But isn't there some way you can stop them?" Walter Lawrence said in desperation.

"Not really, Walter," was Pa's reply. "I checked the man's so-called papers and they seemed all right."

"You mean—"

"That's right, Walter," Pa interrupted. "Unless your customers are using a pistol or a knife to withdraw their funds, there ain't a whole helluva lot I can do."

"Damn." Walter Lawrence almost said it under his breath before remembering there likely weren't any ladies about, so when he got it out of him, why, there was no doubting exactly what it was he'd said.

"Don't worry, Walter," Pa said, placing a firm hand on the man's shoulder, as though that one gesture would return his confidence to him. "At least you got us Carstons. We'll stand by you and the bank."

"True," the banker said as he walked away, "but none of you has much in the way of significant money in my bank either."

"He never was the most grateful man I ever met," Pa said, watching the ramrod-straight figure march back to his bank.

"Ain't no mistaking that, Pa," I said and shook my head with just a tad bit of contempt. I didn't say it to Pa, but in the back of my mind I was thinking that if Walter Lawrence wasn't careful, he wouldn't have a hell of a lot of backing from the Carston clan. Nor would he have our money.

I told Pa I had to get back out to the ranch and headed for my mount again. I was about to climb into the saddle when John Fitch crossed my path again. This time he had a pocketful of cash. I was betting he was on his way to Phineas McDougal's new bank with it and said as much.

"You betcha, George Washington." John confirmed. From the tone in his voice I had a hint he was a man with a purpose in life, with maybe just a touch of greed to go with it. Like I say, money will do that to you. "If you are wise too, you'll take your money and put it in this new bank, my friend."

"I don't know, John," I said with a stammer. "I'd have to think on it. It ain't that we got a lot of money, you understand, it's just that this McDougal fella is awful new to town." What I'd felt about Phineas McDougal was the same thing I figured Pa was feeling, and that was downright suspicious. I didn't want to bust John's bubble, but I had more than my usual doubts about carpetbaggers like McDougal. "You know, John, Pa always said that if the saddle creaks, it ain't paid for."

"Vat's a saddle got to do with a bank account?"

"Maybe nothing," I said with a shrug. "But there's something about this fella that tells me he ain't paid for nothing with his own money in a long time."

"Listen, Wash," John said, pulling out his pocket watch and giving it a glance, "it's almost noon. Let me buy you dinner and tell you how I'm going to make a lot of money with this new bank. Maybe then you'll see the wisdom of what I have in mind."

If it was Chance John had been speaking to, he wouldn't have had to ask twice. Me, well, it was the second time John Fitch was buying me something that morning, and I didn't want to be too beholden to the man, if you know what I mean. But he was insistent about buying me a meal, also mentioning that his wife wanted Chance and me to come out to their place that night for supper, so I gave in and had a noon meal at the Porter Cafe.

As it turned out, John Fitch had met Phineas McDougal in the street after the new banker had finished with his snake-oil salesman's pitch and discussed loans and interest rates. The banker had stood fast to what he'd said and offered John a loan at a relatively low percentage rate and was giving him a full year to repay it. All he had to do was wait a week or so until McDougal had all his bank accounts set up and ready to go and he would be glad to lend John more than he would need to see him through the coming winter season and next spring's planting.

"That sounds like a real good deal, John," I said, having finished my meal while John did most of the talking. "Sounds like you'll make a real profit on that kind of deal."

That was when John went into explaining to me how much money my own savings would make at McDougal's new bank, which was another reason he was taking his money out of Walter Lawrence's bank. If I could save even half of what John was bragging about, I'd make some money by investing in this new bank, of that I was sure. The fact of the matter was, the more I thought about it, with the way Walter Lawrence had treated us Carstons that morning, the more convinced I was that Chance and me needed to put our money in McDougal's new bank.

By two-thirty I had withdrawn our money from the Twin Rifles Bank and Trust and placed it in the Surety Savings and Loan. John Fitch slapped me on the back and wished both of us luck before reminding me again to be at his house with Chance at six o'clock that night for supper.

Chance was sitting in the shady portion of the porch stoop when I returned to the ranch house. Throwing my reins around the hitching rail, I could see he looked dog tired, not to mention dusty. One thing about my brother, when he sets out to do a job, he does that job, and it was clear to me what Chance had spent most of the day doing.

"That old mustang do you in, did he?" I said, figuring that if I acted like I was taking a personal interest in the man and his aches and pains he'd feel a mite better. Sometimes things like that work with a body.

"Not hardly," Chance growled. It was pure effort that made him get up from where he'd set his git-up end, of that much I was sure. Chance Carston wasn't a quitter, not by a long shot. "I reckon we're just sort of wearing one another down."

"Well, I've got some good news."

"What's that?"

I disappeared inside for a moment, setting the sack of flour down where it would be handy the next time I needed it. When I wandered back outside, I said, "John Fitch said his wife wants us over for supper tonight."

Chance ran his sleeve across his forehead and I watched it come away wet with sweat. "Won't have to eat your cooking tonight, huh? That is good news."

"There's more too," I added with a smile.

"Oh?" Chance never was too long on words, so I

could only assume that the easygoing tone of his voice was due to what he'd been experiencing with that wild mustang.

"Yeah." I then proceeded to tell him, in as short a version as possible, of Phineas McDougal's arrival in town and the commotion it had stirred in opening up a new bank. Before he could ask me what was so good about that, I finished by saying, "I closed out our account with Old Man Lawrence and opened a new account with Phineas McDougal's Surety Savings and Loan."

Like I said, Chance can be short on words a lot. At first I thought the meanness that screwed up in his face was the same as that he'd felt toward the mustang, but I soon found out different. It was a hell of a lot worse. He turned his head sideways, the way a dog will when he's looking at you like you've done something totally out of this world, altogether unreasonable. I was standing full on his left side now, so I didn't see him drop his hat, not until it was too late.

"You stupid ass," I heard my brother growl, but before I could wonder why, he had knocked me ass over teakettle with a hard right that sent me rolling over in the dirt a time or two.

"What the hell'd you do that for?" I said, bringing blood away from my mouth, although I could tell what it was by the taste of it long before I saw it. That was my first mistake. I'd gotten to my feet and took a swipe at my cut lip.

"That's my money too, you damn fool!" Chance all but yelled and took another swing at me. I don't know about you, hoss, but I never liked being taken for a fool more than once. I ducked under my brother's blow, knowing it was a hard one by the swoosh of air I felt about me. Still, there was a feeling of relief in knowing that I hadn't been hit that time. The thing was, I wasn't about to be beaten up by my older brother—again.

He put everything into that swing and lost his balance when he didn't connect with his target. Me, I didn't plan on giving my brother another chance to hit me, so I hit him hard in the side twice, once with my left as he went off balance, a second time with my right as he staggered forward some. I may not be as big and strong as Chance, but I make up for it with being quick, and I did a good deal of that right then. I do believe that if it hadn't been for that old mustang wearing my brother out like it had, Chance would have gotten back up and killed me then and there. But I kicked him square in the ass while I had him off guard and he fell on his side, staying there for a minute to catch his breath while I stood over him and gave him the same ugly look he'd given me not two minutes ago.

"What the hell's got into you, Chance?" I said, although I knew I was asking a useless question.

"Ain't that account in *both* our names?" he said, coughing up something and spitting it out.

"Yeah, I just thought—"

"Thinking ain't your long suit today, is it, little brother?" He was standing at his full height now, maybe an inch taller than me, but the way he stretched that inch you'd have thought it was ten feet. "You was dead wrong, Wash. You should've talked to me about that account before you closed it out. Don't ever do it to me again, understand?"

"You made yourself clear," I said and retreated to the house.

In a minute I heard Chance cussing something fierce again. He'd thrown the reins on old Nightmare again and climbed on, only to be thrown to the ground. I saw him sitting there in the dust, shaking his head in despair, and decided I was a mite mad too.

I made my way out to the corral, climbed over the rails, then climbed on old Nightmare. By that time Chance had hauled his carcass out of the way, likely making room for me when I dusted my britches not far from where he'd landed.

But it gave Chance a breather, at least for a minute or two. By then he must have felt froggy enough to climb back up on the mustang and have at it.

It was plain to see that we were both working out our frustrations on that wild mustang, both determined to tame the horse. The fact of the matter is we did tame it. Yes sir. After three hours of steady climbing on and getting thrown off that horse, Old Nightmare wasn't a nightmare anymore. Mind you, he had a lot of gentling to do yet, but he wasn't near as ornery as the horse I'd seen my brother climb on that morning.

I couldn't tell you about Chance, but I almost preferred walking over to John Fitch's to riding that evening.

CHAPTER
★ 5 ★

John Fitch had two children. Stephen was his eight-year-old boy and Marie his fourteen-year-old girl. They had a real treat that night, especially when they saw Chance riding old Nightmare up to the gate. We'd both done our best to clean up for this invite to a supper meal, but from the looks on the faces of those kids, why, we could have come buck naked and they wouldn't have noticed. They were that interested in the mustang my brother was riding.

I reckon you could say Nightmare had gone from being flat-out wild to a mite more than frisky that day. Or maybe that was because Chance rode a lot of it out of the mustang on the way over to the Fitch place that night.

"Well, what do you think, Marie?" Chance said, climbing down from the saddle.

"Oh, he's beautiful," the young girl said in admiration. She could have been describing herself, I thought, for it wouldn't be long before she'd be turning into a fine-looking young filly too. Part of the growing, I'd noticed, was taking a liking to Chance and damn near everything he did or said. If Marie thought old Nightmare was a beauty, she held the same line of thought about Chance. She just wasn't saying. But then she didn't have too.

"He's yours too," Chance said with a smile.

Marie's eyes got wide with surprise and her mouth dropped open far enough so you'd doubt she'd ever get it hinged and closed again.

"Really? You're kidding," she blurted out before running to meet her mama, who was coming out the front door. "He's mine, Mama, he's mine! Chance gave him to me! Isn't he beautiful?"

Greta Fitch might have been pushing forty, but she sure didn't look it. The fact is, she didn't look an awful lot like her husband at all. Where John was stout, Greta was well proportioned, what my brother likes to call healthy. There was a good deal of life in her blue eyes, which seemed to sparkle like a spring creek full of ice water. The thing I cautioned myself about with this woman was the reddish tint to her hair, which made it auburn in color, I reckon. I've run across more than my share of redheaded women in my life and there wasn't a one of them that didn't carry a good deal of fire within her once she got crossed. I reckon if there was one thing about the couple that seemed to shine, it would have to have been the love of life they felt that was evident in how they'd brought up their children.

"My, but he is a beautiful one indeed, my child," Greta said, taking in the horse as Chance still held the reins. "But you can't be serious about giving Marie a horse. She is much too young."

"Nonsense," Chance said. "Why, me and Wash learned to ride before we could walk."

"And shoot before you could talk," Greta said in a chiding way. "Yes, I know how you frontier boys are."

"Can we ride him?" Marie asked excitedly.

"As long as your ma and pa say it's all right," Chance said.

"All right," Greta said, giving Chance a playful frown. "But you," she added, pointing to Chance, "must go with her to ensure her safety."

"We won't be long," my brother said, and the two were soon gone, Chance riding his horse right along with Marie.

"What about me?" Stephen asked in a low, shameful voice. I'd seen sad-eyed hound dogs that looked happier than this boy right now.

"Oh, you ain't been forgot, Stephen," I said, and I guaranteed the boy that he'd be able to ride old Nightmare just as much as his sister. "Of course, I saved the important stuff for you."

"You did?" His disposition immediately perked up.

"Why sure. See, I know you're a responsible sort, so I'm counting on you to make sure old Nightmare gets taken care of proper," I said. "Believe me, Stephen, there ain't an animal or a human that ever forgot where his food come from. You take care of that hoss proper and you'll have a friend for life."

Mind you, what I'd passed on to the boy wasn't as good as being given a present, but given responsibility in those days had its own reward, so he didn't shirk the duty I'd handed him and rushed off to tell his pa about it.

Greta had cooked up a fancy stew for supper. She kept saying it wasn't much, but the rest of us ate it up like it was our last supper. I'd found out a long time back that food always tastes better when someone else is fixing it for you. It tastes real good if that someone can cook better than average, and Greta was one whale of a cook.

Chance made little mention of what he thought of me taking our money and putting it in Phineas McDougal's new bank, even when John started telling him how great were the plans he had for the future. After the meal, Chance took the kids out to the barn to show them how to curry down old Nightmare good and proper. Greta poured us all more coffee and I sat back, wondering if I could ever stuff myself this full again.

"You know, John, I always have wondered how you come by this spread," I said shortly. "I always thought those German folk settled with their own over Mayville way."

"Many have," John said, "many have."

"But not Hans," Greta said with a smile and a good deal of pride. "My Hans is different from them all. To be an American, that is his goal."

"Nothing wrong with that," I said.

"No," John agreed. "But sometimes a man must gamble—'buck the tiger' is how your river-rat gamblers put it, eh?"

"Yeah, I reckon so."

Greta set about cleaning off the table, as though she knew it was time for the men to talk and she to go about her chores. Still, I knew she heard everything we said, so I made it a point of watching my language.

"You know, Wash, you Americans are not the only ones who can tell a story. 'Spin a yarn,' isn't that how you say it?"

"Yeah."

"So you vant to know how I came by all this, eh?"

I nodded and took a sip of coffee.

"Vell, let me tell you a story, my friend," John began. "It all starts in Prussia where, just as in your country, things are not alvays vat they seem. Even in the old country they fight duels, and in this case an unpopular man von."

According to John's story, the man had to leave the country right quick and at the time the only ships available were headed for Mexico, a country that was receptive to new people at the time. John called the man in his story Von Roeder and painted a picture of the man as rather aggressive, not to mention being one hell of a card player.

Von Roeder, once he got to Mexico, was a bit of a roamer and went to making his living with cards and such. One day he met up with a braggart of sorts who also proved to be a landowner in those parts. John called him Wales.

The two men sat in on a card game that started out with half a dozen men but was soon down to Von Roeder and Wales. As it turned out, Wales might have been good at running his mouth, but he had little luck with cards. Wales was soon out of cash and began writing out bills of sale on the animals he owned. Von Roeder soon owned several cows, horses, pigs, and hens. Those who had gathered to watch the game began to caution Wales about proceeding any farther.

"No, I will not quit!" the landowner said loudly. "My luck cannot stay this bad much longer."

They continued to play, Von Roeder giving his adversary the chance to reclaim his money and animals. But Wales's luck ran no better and he was soon betting—and losing—tools and machinery that were used on his farm. In one final desperate play to win, he bet the deed to the farm.

And lost.

"It is time to quit," Von Roeder said with a smile. "You have nothing left to bet with, my friend."

"Wait," Wales said, and he left the table for a minute. What he returned with were a beautiful young lady and a piece of paper. "Here, sir, is my wife and our marriage license. I'll bet it on one final hand."

Von Roeder was taken with this young woman's beauty and smiled at her, noticing that she willingly returned his smile. "Only with the lady's permission," he said.

When the woman nodded her head, the cards were dealt one last time and Wales drew a hand that was just as bad as the rest of the cards he'd played that day. By this time, Wales was anything but a gracious loser and he drew one of the pistols he carried and fired at Von Roeder. His luck seemed little better with firearms than with cards, for he missed Von Roeder, who by then had a rapier in his hand. Von Roeder ran it through Wales's heart, killing him on the spot.

Once again Von Roeder was in trouble, for Wales

proved to be a popular man in the territory. So he sold the farm and animals and tools.

John paused for a moment in silence, taking a sip of his coffee. He'd gotten my attention with his story.

"What happened to the woman?" I asked.

"He married her and took her north with him when he crossed the Rio Grande and settled down in Texas," Greta said with a smile. "Some say she had red hair and blue eyes and a wild disposition," she added, and I swear that she was blushing when she spoke.

"So that's how you come on buying this place, huh?" I said, drinking the last of my coffee.

"Oh, no," John said. "It's just a way that some have used to get by in coming to America. Some men of difficulty, let us say."

"Then how did you come to settle here?"

"Oh, it is of little importance," John said and seemed to want to let it go at that.

Chance and the kids came back into the house, the two youngsters hanging on every word Chance was saying.

"Now you know how to take care of old Nightmare properly, right?" my brother said.

"Yes, sir," both kids replied in unison.

"And nobody fights over him, right?"

"Yes, sir." It was clear Chance was enjoying whatever role he was playing immensely. For a man who'd had a frown on his face all day, he was full of smiles now and happy as a lark.

"Good, it's settled," Chance said. He then paused for a moment in thought, before adding, "Of course, if your mama or daddy see you not keeping up with your chores and schoolwork, I expect they'll let me know and I'll come take old Nightmare back."

"Oh, no, Chance," Marie said in as honest a face as I've ever seen on a young girl her age, "Stephen and I will do it all, just like you say."

"Right," the boy said in agreement.

"Good," Chance said, concluding their deal with a comfortable smile. To me, he said, "I reckon we'd better be getting back home, Wash. It's getting dark."

I nodded and thanked Greta for the fine meal we'd been invited to, then followed Chance out to our horses. John's story was still heavy on my mind as we mounted up.

"Say, Chance," I said, curiosity getting the best of me, "is that a rapier I saw over John's fireplace? I disremember."

My brother pushed back his hat and scratched his head, thinking. He smiled before saying, "I do believe it is one of those King Arthur swords they went around sticking people with in John's old country. Why do you ask, little brother?"

"Oh, nothing, nothing at all," I said. "But Chance?"

"Yeah," he said, getting ready to lay the reins across that horse of his.

"I wouldn't play cards with old John."

"Oh?"

"Yeah. I don't think he takes kindly to sore losers."

Like I said, it was one hell of a day.

CHAPTER
★ 6 ★

John Fitch and me weren't the only ones who opened new accounts with Phineas McDougal and his bank. I wasn't in town more than half an hour the next day before I found out that there weren't more than a dozen accounts left in Walter Lawrence's Twin Rifles Bank and Trust. I didn't have to ask to find out that most of those were old-timers who'd been in Twin Rifles the longest, one of whom was Pa. And he was critical of all the rest of us.

"You folks made a big mistake," Pa said, shaking a finger at me when the subject came up at his office. I got the distinct impression that he was determined to be a burr under my saddle—and anyone else who'd changed their bank account within the last twenty-four hours. "You ain't old enough to remember the depression of '37," he continued in a preachy way, still shaking his finger like some schoolteacher upset with his students. "Why, money was so tight then—"

"I know, Pa, I know. I'd have had better chances of squeezing blood out of a turnip," I said, repeating what I suspicioned he'd say. One thing about the man you call your father: After several years you can pretty much tell what kind of ways he takes to expressing himself. If yours is anything like mine, he's got a certain way of palavering on specific subjects with a distinct set of words. With Pa it was usually getting some sort of ungettable thing from something else just as unlikely, like blood and turnips. "But you've got to remember, Pa, this ain't 1837 anymore."

"Well, ary you knew spit about the economy, you'd sure as hell know what a depression felt like," he added, giving me a hard look for daring to back talk him.

"What in the world are you two arguing about now?" The words came from Pa's deputy, who had walked in during our discussion. Joshua was a new addition to Twin Rifles when I'd returned from the war. He hadn't been there when Chance and I had gone off to war, but Pa had taken him on as a deputy since then. I'd met some men like Joshua during the war, men who'd wandered out of the hills from back in Tennessee or Kentucky and had discovered civilization but had the good sense to remember their own set of values. I'd taken a shine to Joshua for managing to mix a sense of humor with most of what he said.

"Aw, it's that damn bank," Pa grumbled, the furrow in his brow growing deeper than when he'd first begun preaching to me.

"Don't blame you one whit, Will," Joshua said. "Why, I can remember when I didn't have nothing but a shirt and pants. Feller give me a pair of boots one day in late fall and I put 'em on my hands to keep warm."

"Hell, Joshua, I got a notion they didn't discover clothes where you come from until they learned how to kill a deer," Pa said, only half in jest. Still, it gave me a chuckle.

"Now don't you laugh too hard, young man," Joshua said, a serious look about him now. Trouble was you couldn't always tell whether his serious look was serious or just a front for some back-home philosophy. With cocked eyebrow, he added, "Why, before Will Carston give me this job, I wasn't doing much more'n making my way from sunup to sundown and doing it with what little gunpowder I had. Your daddy give me a good job and a decent amount of money to live off 'un in a month's time." It was true enough, for Joshua was getting all of twenty dollars a month as a deputy. Of course, Pa got all of forty or fifty dollars a month plus the few extra dollars he pulled in as a deputy United States marshal, so he wasn't starving.

"Hell, Joshua, all you do is sit around and drink coffee and run a few errands for Pa," I said with as straight a face as I could manage.

As I expected, Joshua was taken aback by my words. He jerked his head back as though I'd nailed him with a right cross and was trying to do him in. Then a cloud formed on his forehead and a devilish mean look came over him as he frowned at me.

"My eye and Betty Martin! Wash, I'm gonna take that as a misguided poke at me and my position, little as it is around here," he said, taking a step closer to me. Like I said, a lot of time you can't tell what's going on inside this man's mind, so I didn't know what to expect. For all I knew I could have hit one of the man's tender spots. It happens, you know. "Jest don't you forget that when the time comes, I've been more than ready to lay my life on the line. And you of all people should know that."

"I'm sure he does," Pa said, stepping between us. I'll tell you, hoss, I sure did feel a might of relief when Pa did that. "Wash was just funning you. After all, he's done some badge toting his own self."

"Yeah," I said with a gulp, suddenly aware of how dry my throat was. "Can't you take a little joshing?" How could I ever forget that Pa had been a Texas Ranger in this land most of the youth of Chance and me? Why, he'd had us sworn in as soon as he thought we were old enough to use horse sense and accompany him on some of his missions. The Rangers hadn't been in existence since 1863 or so and had yet to make a comeback in Texas, but once you'd been a Texas Ranger it was hard to ever forget the law and order you were supposed to stand for in that position. Even now, after spending four rather unruly years as a Confederate soldier, I still knew the code, still knew what it represented, not to mention what I represented. Thinking back on it, I had come to the conclusion one day that the Texas Rangers had made bringing us up kind of easy for Pa. Shoot, all he had to do was swear us in and tell us what we had to do to uphold the law. You didn't get much better a view of common sense and fair play than the code a Ranger had to use in determining what he had to do next. Yes, I'd toted a badge for a while before going off to war.

"Speaking of running errands," Pa said to Joshua, "have you got your horse ready to ride?"

"You betcha, Will. That's why I stopped in, to see if there was anything else you wanted me to do on the way to the circus."

"No. You just get there and check out this McDougal fella and git back here quick as you can before he steals these people blind." Pa gave Joshua a confident wink and a nod, and the man was gone just as quickly.

"Checking on the new banker, are you?" I asked as I heard Joshua's horse heading out of town.

"Part of my job is keeping the unsavory element out of town," Pa said, "and I consider Phineas McDougal to be unsavory at best."

The "circus," as Joshua had put it, was the nearest big city, in this case San Antonio. Big cities offered country people like Joshua just as much as any circus they'd ever see in their lifetime, so calling a big city the circus didn't seem too far out of line. The reason Pa had to send Joshua to the nearest big city was to get the use of the closest telegraph. The telegraph companies had made a big production of putting the Pony Express out of business about the fall of '61 when they hooked up and were able to send messages from San Francisco to Washington and New York in a mere matter of seconds. The trouble with all of that was it took them a while to branch out to the north and south of that main line they'd stretched across the plains of Kansas and across the Rocky Mountains. Once they did, they initially only put up enough pole and wire to the main cities, so the smaller towns like Twin Rifles were left without any fancy telegraph service. That meant that whenever he needed to use the quickness of the telegraph, Pa had to get word to San Antonio, where the nearest facility was set up. And right now Pa thought Phineas McDougal important enough a subject to send a wire to Austin.

"It'll take a couple of days for Joshua to make it there and back, but I've got a notion I'm not going to be surprised at what I find out about that man," Pa said. He rubbed a hand across his jaw, as though in thought, before saying, "That man's slipperier than an eel, I tell you."

"I don't know, Pa. John Fitch seemed convinced the man was going to be able to help him pay off his taxes and get his farm back to a paying proposition again. The man knows how to handle his money, I'd say."

"Wash," Pa said, "if John Fitch knew how to handle his money, why, he wouldn't be as broke as the rest of the farmers around here, would he?"

I shrugged. Like I say, money matters never was my long suit.

"Besides, you put the smell of money up before a man and he's likely to lose his money and everything else for all the greed that's running through his mind." Pa seemed awful confident about what he was saying, and maybe he was right. Maybe this man was going to wind up taking us for everything we had. But I'll tell you what, hoss, the thought of not being constantly on the verge of being poor was a real pleasurable one.

Whether Pa realized it or not, it had a good deal of appeal to a good share of the rest of the townspeople in Twin Rifles.

CHAPTER
★ 7 ★

If you want to live for any amount of time, there are three questions you never ask a stranger in Texas: "Why did you leave home?" "Where do you come from?" "Where did you get your horse?" Any one of the three is a sure sign of asking for trouble. Asking any two of the questions, especially in the same breath, is an indication that although you may not be faint of heart, you may soon find yourself wishing you were. If you have the courage—or stupidity—to ask all three within the space of thirty seconds, well, you might also find it advisable to have a coffin and plot laid out with the local carpenter or undertaker.

This is not idle chatter, as might be expected from the town gossip or some old-timer sitting around with a jug and a passel of stories to tell. Ever since the end of the war there had been a whole collection of strangers invading Texas, orphans of the war in one form or another. It was often hard telling who they were and what they were. I had always been fair about the whole thing and tried not to judge my fellow man, hoping he would have the same kind of respect for me. After all, some of these fellows might make good cowhands or be willing to work at whatever job they could find. But some, as Pa claimed, had likely run afoul of the law and lacked desire to find honest work in the first place. Pa, Chance, and I had already had one such run-in to prove the validity of Pa's theory, but that's a whole 'nother canyon.

The trouble with most of these drifters was that we kept seeing more of them who had indeed run afoul of the law, or something or someone else, and were on the run than we did the honest ones looking for a decent job. This usually explained why they were just "passing through" and stopped only long enough to wet their whistle and pick up a few supplies—if they had the money to pay for them. So asking them why they'd left home, where they'd come from, and where they picked up that horse they were riding was more than an invitation to tangle with a potentially bad man. If you weren't careful you could wind up dead.

I kept all that in mind when I returned to Twin Rifles a couple of days later and noticed that there were some strange horses at the hitching post outside Ernie Johnson's saloon. Pa was right about one thing: When people get to dealing with money and the temptation of profit, why, it becomes an obsession with them. Unfortunately, they also take to gabbing about it so much that the word spreads like wildfire, no matter where you happen to be. Seeing those extra horses made me wonder if the rest of Texas hadn't heard about Phineas McDougal and his bank and were making tracks to our fair town.

"Twice in one week, Wash," Ernie said when I stepped up to the bar in the welcome coolness inside the saloon. It was late in the morning, not long past the time Ernie Johnson usually opened up, and I was surprised at the amount of customers he already had. "Must be some kind of record."

"No," I said with a smile. "This time I'm doing it the smart way. I ain't making my visit to the general store until I get good and ready to leave town." I'd made the last of the coffee before riding in to town, knowing all too well that coffee was one of the staples of the frontier and that my brother would be even more intolerable than he was now if he didn't have good strong coffee to make it through the rest of the day.

"There you go," Ernie said, returning the smile, likely remembering the fracas I'd gotten into over John Fitch a couple of days before. When he set a beer down before me, he added, "John Fitch says it's on him," and he pointed toward the end of the bar where John was enjoying his beer.

I took the moment to notice that between John and me were the four men I assumed belonged to the horses out front. Only one of them still had any semblance of a uniform on, and he seemed the biggest of the bunch. He was easily as tall as Chance and near his build, big in the shoulders and chest with hands that, when made into a fist, probably looked like small

Too Many Drifters

hams. The front of his hat was pushed back the way I'd seen some old cavalry sergeants do, either from riding into the wind or from fashioning it that way. His face was weatherbeaten, his nose only slightly out of place. I was betting he'd seen his fair share of fights and come out on top of most.

"Still in the cavalry, Sarge, or were you just too lively for 'em?" I said with a grin, hoping he'd take it the way I meant it. The blue Union uniform was about as beaten as the man's face, but what showed most on it now was the dark background of the shoulder sleeve where once sergeant stripes had been worn. Did he get out of the army with most of the rest of his type? Or was he still in the cavalry and only a man who had been busted in rank? Believe me, friend, I knew I was getting dangerously close to asking those three unthinkable questions. At the same time I knew that I had money in a newly established bank with the rest of the town and didn't want it withdrawn by anyone other than myself.

The man took a sip of his beer and smiled at me in a friendly way. "Well, son, I reckon it was a bit of both." I never did care for being called son by anyone other than Pa, but this man was somewhere between Chance and Pa in the age department, so I didn't make a fuss over it.

"Wash Carston's the name."

"Emmett," he said and nodded to me by way of introduction, adding, "Mind telling me just what it is that made you ask that question?" Mind you now, I've had more than one fight with my brother, and they've been rough and tough ones, so fighting this fellow wouldn't be any different. But there was the money in the bank to be considered, so I tried being as tactful as possible.

"Nothing really," I said with a shrug. Then, seeing that wouldn't do for an answer, I said, "It's just that I recall a season or so back running across some fellas who'd been riding army mounts who wound up coming to a sad end."

"Is that so?" he said and raised a suspicious eyebrow.

"Turned out they were deserters and there was a U.S. marshal chasing 'em. Caught up with 'em and didn't do a helluva lot of discussing over the matter."

"I see," Emmett said, draining the contents of his glass.

"Fact is he killed 'em dead as could be."

"Sounds like a dangerous man. Got a name, does he?"

"Hickok," I said, looking in his eyes to see what kind of reaction I'd get. "Wild Bill Hickok." When one of Emmett's riding pards gave a low whistle, I knew that the man I'd briefly known as Wild Bill Hickok wasn't just bragging about his exploits during the War Between the States. His reputation had apparently gotten around.

"I think he's back in Missouri some place," I said, as though the words would assure these men they were safe from the lawman's presence in Twin Rifles.

"Well, don't you worry, Mr. Carston," Emmett said. "I paid twenty dollars of my mustering-out pay for that horse out front. If you need proof, I can dig it out of my saddlebag for you." He paused then, reaching over and thumbing back the cowhide vest he wore as though looking for something in particular.

"Of course, it's usually the local law that takes to asking those questions. And I don't see no badge on you."

"I'm not looking for any trouble, Mr. Emmett," I said. "Just passing along some free advice."

"I'll keep that in mind," was his reply.

John Fitch bought the four drifters each another beer and they thanked him profusely. Of course, if I'd been on a dusty trail for a long time, I reckon I'd be appreciative of a free beer too—even if it was slightly warm.

My experiences with the inside of a saloon didn't seem of the quiet nature of late. It didn't change when Pardee Taylor came busting into the saloon a few minutes later. He appeared to already be roaring drunk, and you could safely assume that the man was looking for trouble. It was just his way. Drunk or sober, he seemed to search it out.

"Out of my way, you goddamn Kraut!" he said after making his way to the far end of the bar and pushing John Fitch to the wall.

"Don't start it, Pardee," I heard Ernie Johnson say in as demanding a voice as he could muster. Unlike many barkeeps I'd seen, Ernie was rather smallish in size and easygoing. It usually took a lot to get him riled before he'd take any kind of action. "I'll get Will Carston to put you in jail where you belong." On the other hand, getting your bar busted up by the likes of this man was enough to draw anyone's ire.

"Shut up and give me a bottle, Johnson," Pardee growled, his drunkenness bringing out the mean in him.

John Fitch had gotten up and tapped Pardee on the

shoulder. When the drunk turned his way, John laid a hard right fist across his face, knocking him back into one of the remaining drifters. When the man tried to do something about it, Pardee backhanded him and went for his gun.

It was a mistake.

Emmett had pushed himself away from the bar, going for his pistol as he did. When Pardee had his six-gun out, Emmett had already drawn and cocked his Colt Army Model .44. Believe me, friend, nothing will get your attention more than a rifle or a six-gun being cocked in the same room you're in. Especially if all you can do is hear it and not see it. It purely makes you wonder who in the devil that big gun is aimed at, for if it's *you,* why, you're in real trouble.

"I wouldn't do that if I was you," Emmett said in a no-nonsense tone of voice.

Pardee Taylor froze on the spot, his back to the man. He had the gun out before him now, barrel pointed straight up in the air. He could shoot John Fitch before him, which was his full intent, or try wheeling and shooting the man now giving him orders. From the sheer indecision of the man, I had the distinct notion that Pardee Taylor had sobered up real quick like.

"I'd listen to him, Pardee," I said with a grin. "Looks to me like his pistol's loaded and all. Yes sir, I'd listen to him."

"I could kill you, mister," Pardee said, trying to sound braver than I knew he was.

"Emmett. You call me Emmett. As for killing me, you ain't drunk or sober enough, sonny." There was a chuckle from some of the patrons in the saloon before

Emmett added, "Besides, the man you want to shoot is buying me beer. Do you know how hard it is to come by free beer these days? Spoil my day, it would."

"Gentlemen, I think you'd both better take it outside of this saloon, not to mention out of my town ary you want to do any shooting." It was Pa who was talking now from the batwing doors of the saloon entrance. And he had one of his Remingtons in hand, ready for any kind of business these two men would care to discuss.

Both must have realized there was no percentage in what they had in mind and slowly lowered their guns and holstered them.

"Taylor," Pa said, as though talking to a child in a stern manner, "don't even bother finishing your drink. Just slosh on your hat, plant your sorry ass on that nag you call a horse, and get out of town. Now!"

Pardee Taylor did just that, brushing past Emmett, me, and Pa with one of the most hateful looks I've ever seen in my life.

"I keep telling you, Wash, I can't pull you out of these scrapes forever," Pa said and just as quickly was gone.

"Handle yourself pretty well," Ernie Johnson said as he set up another round of beer for the four drifters and myself.

"From what I understand, a man's got to in this part of the country," Emmett said with a sly grin.

"You said there was some kind of complications involved with you leaving the army?" I asked, again trying to be cautious in choosing my words.

The former sergeant took a pull on his beer before turning his gaze toward me. "Truth is there was," he said. "Busted a sergeant major's jaw and put his colonel out of commission when he tried to interrupt. I hate to be interrupted."

I smiled, figuring I'd likely get along with this man. "I know what you mean."

"There a reason you're all of a sudden taking a personal interest in my life?" Emmett asked.

"If you're looking for a job, yes."

"What kind?" Emmett asked, after looking at his friends, then back at me.

It was at this point that I explained that me and my brother had a small ranch outside town, were in the process of breaking some horses, and that we had an army contract to deliver them as soon as they were in riding condition.

"Don't know as I'd be any good at it," Emmett said after a few minutes of thought on the subject. With a smile, he added, "Of course, I've had more than my fair share of mustangs to ride during the war."

"I can't offer you much in the line of pay, at least not until we sell the horses," I said. "But you'll have a roof over your head and three squares a day for your efforts."

"What do you think, boys?" he then asked the three men with him.

"Sure beats cadging drinks," one of them said.

"Well, Mr. Carston, looks like you've got four horse busters," Emmett said, a slight grin growing on his face.

"Good," I said and stuck out my paw. He took it in a hardy manner, and I knew his fists would be as big as hams, just like I first figured. "I've got to pick up some coffee at the general store. You finish your beers and be ready to ride in ten or fifteen minutes."

"You've got a deal."

I headed for the door, then stopped and spoke to the man over my shoulder. "Oh, Mr. Emmett, that foofaraw you got into with that sergeant major and colonel: They bust you for it, did they?"

Emmett smiled, remembering the past. "Oh yeah, three or four times in as many years."

I smiled, more to myself than anyone else, before leaving. "That's what I thought," I said.

CHAPTER
★ 8 ★

Bond, McHale, and Compton. Those were the names of Emmett's saddle pards. The four of them had made a meal of the free lunch Ernie Johnson put out on his bar about noon or so each day, so I didn't have to worry about feeding them right off. I figured that Chance would at least be glad about that.

"That fella with the downcast look about him is my brother," I said as we approached our ranch house. Chance looked about as dissatisfied now as he had when I'd left earlier in the morning. He must have run out of coffee and staying power with whichever bronc he had been trying to break.

"I hope you didn't bring home company for supper," he growled as I dismounted at the hitching rail. "I ain't in the mood for palavering."

"He's never in the mood for palavering," I said to the new crew with half a smile. "Chance, this is Emmett, Bond, McHale, and Compton."

"Howdy," each man said in his own voice, giving a nod or a tip of the hat to my brother.

"Do tell," was all Chance could muster in words.

"I take it this is one of your bad days," Emmett said, trying on a grin for size. At least he was trying to get off to a good start.

I made sure I was a good dozen feet away from Chance before I said, "They're gonna help us break these mustangs, Chance."

"What?" My brother frowned at me, the look on his face saying he would have swung at me good and hard had I been within distance. But he seemed too damned tired to even try now. I figured out about halfway home that I'd likely run into this problem again, me having the audacity to do something that had to do with our partnership in this ranch without consulting my brother. Yesterday it was changing banks, today it was hiring these men without so much as a parley with Chance. Neither one set well with my brother, of that I was sure.

"I got some Arbuckle's too," I said, hoping I could discourage him from starting trouble with these new hands. But Chance only squinted his eyes as he stared at each from top to bottom.

"Yankee, huh?" he said to Emmett. "You might do. What about the rest? Rebel or Yank?"

"Does it matter?" Emmett said, as though speaking for the rest.

"Don't mind Chance," I said, feeling a mite skittish about the whole thing now. Before Chance could insult them anymore, I added, "We took on four men about a year ago when we started this ranch. They stole our horses. Had to chase 'em down into Mexico before we caught 'em."

"Looks like you got your horses back," Emmett said, glancing past us at the corral.

"What'd you do to 'em when you caught 'em?" Bond asked.

"Down in these parts they hang horse thieves," Chance said in his meanest voice. "Me, I shot 'em outright."

If impressing these men was what my brother had in mind, he pretty much succeeded, for each raised his eyebrows in astonishment. Truth be known, my brother hadn't killed any of the horse thieves, although he now implied to the contrary. The four men, Confederates who had originally been with General Shelby on his way into Mexico, had actually helped us defend our town once we'd returned to Twin Rifles and had died in that process.

"I explained to them that they wouldn't get paid until we sold the horses," I said. "They're agreeable to that." Somehow or another, I could feel a fight coming on, no matter what I would say.

"Well now, you're a tough hombre, ain't you?" Emmett said and stood there, hands on his hips, the look on his face none too pleasant.

Chance, he wasn't about to be bluffed. "That's right, mister. And I'll do the same thing to any one of the four of you who takes anything off this ranch, especially a horse."

Too Many Drifters

Emmett took a quick step forward and threw a roundhouse punch that caught my brother right on the jaw, sending him flying back ass over breakfast.

"Never accuse a man of stealing something unless you've got the evidence to prove it, sonny," he said with a growl as Chance got to his feet, a new sort of energy coming to my brother now.

Chance swung and missed as Emmett ducked under his blow and kicked him in the thigh, again sending my brother to the ground. Chance never was a good loser, so I knew he was thinking on the ground this time. Emmett took a step closer and my brother rolled on his side and brought his foot straight out, kicking Emmett's leg out from under him. The exsergeant reached down for his ankle, which must have smarted, giving Chance the time he needed to get back on his feet and throw the punches he wanted.

This time it was Emmett who landed on the ground. But he was no mindless heathen, like some big men. His mind was working too, and he pulled the same maneuver on Chance that had worked for my brother, kicking out a foot of his own and striking Chance on his ankle, which set him to hopping about.

When he was on his feet, Emmett was close enough to land a blow to Chance's face, causing him to reel back into a thick wood post, one of the two holding up the roof on our small veranda. But he also made a mistake, for when he threw a straight punch at my brother's head, Chance ducked and Emmett slammed his fist into the hard wood. Both of them were jumping about now, so I walked between them and pushed them apart, both landing on their keisters not three feet apart, facing each other.

The three new hands had a good laugh out of it all.

"This ain't no way to get work done, fellas," I said, but I had a notion they didn't hear a word I was saying.

"What rank were you?" Emmett asked, out of breath.

"Sergeant," Chance replied, just as out of breath.

"Cavalry?"

"Betcherass."

"We oughtta get along fine." A big grin came to Emmett's face as he stuck out his paw. Chance had just as big a grin on his face as he took this new man's hand in his own.

"I'm gonna make some coffee," I said, probably to myself, and I left the two sitting where they were, reminiscing about old times that weren't too long ago.

After I'd stoked the pot-bellied stove and tossed some Arbuckle's in the coffeepot, I wandered back outside. What I saw made me feel kind of proud of myself. Mind you, Chance might have been right as rain in being mad at me for changing our bank account without talking it over with him, but he looked like he was getting along fine with these new men.

"And the sooner we get these mustangs broke and in riding shape, the sooner all of us will get paid for our efforts, gents," Chance was saying to them near the corral.

"Then let's get to it, mister," Emmett said and undid his gunbelt and set it aside in a gentle manner, tossing his worn-looking cavalry hat on top of both belt and gun when he was through. "Ain't no use in wearing what's gonna come off anyway on this kind of ride," he added, as though by way of explanation, just in case anyone had it in mind to ask. To Chance, he said, "Let's get to work, brother."

Everyone climbed up on the corral we were using to do our bronc busting in, setting their git-up end on the top rung and hitching a boot on the next rung down to keep their balance. They could have come to see the circus and they wouldn't have been more pleased. At least for right now. I had a distinct notion that my brother was going to make sure each had a chance to give these wild critters a ride before the afternoon was out.

Chance threw a loop around the frog hopper he'd apparently been riding earlier, quickly wrapped the length of rope around a big hardwood post in the center of the corral, and dug his heels into the ground, fighting with every bit of energy to keep the mustang from winning out over him. He'd already made certain the horse was saddled, an effort I knew was considerable since I'd had to do this chore too. Experience had taught me that it was one of the less pleasurable tasks to be done around here.

"Whoa now, boy," my brother was saying gently as the horse stood still and listened to his soothing voice. "Ain't no one gonna hurt you now." He gave the big animal a soft pet, the way I imagined he would a dog, if he owned one.

Meanwhile, Emmett had worked his way around to the horse's side, running a callused hand over its neck and down its foreleg. "You've got an eye for horseflesh, son, I'll give you that," Emmett said with what I thought to be a good deal of respect. But then horsemen usually act that way toward one another. "What is he, twenty hands?"

"That's what I figure." Chance slowly released the rope from the horse's neck, still holding him firm, still baby talking him. "You ready to ride?"

"Might's well."

Just as Emmett reached for the saddle horn to pull himself into the saddle, Chance bought him some time. My brother quickly bent over to his side but a few inches and took a good healthy bite of the horse's ear. I knew this would take the horse's mind off the fact that there was a man almost as wild as he boarding him now, but I also knew the act would give Emmett one hellacious ride.

It did just that.

Chance turned tail and ran hell for leather for our position on the corral as the wild mustang took to bucking as soon as Emmett's tail set down in that saddle. The real wild ones took to what you call frog hopping, arching their back as high as possible while they tried to touch their front hooves with their back. It was enough to rattle any man's bones, and I counted to ten before Emmett went soaring into the air, dusting his set britches and rolling out of the way as the horse bucked on past him.

"Whew!" he said when he got to our side, trying unsuccessfully to rid his trousers of the massive amount of dust they seemed to have accumulated. "That one's a real hell raiser."

"Not bad," Chance said without emotion.

"I'll tell you what, mister," I said with a smile, "you're doing twice as good as I did my first time on one of those critters. Why, I wasn't in the saddle but five seconds before I bit the dust. You lasted all of ten."

"Rattle your bones, he will," Emmett said, gazing at the mustang with what I thought was a whole new respect for the animal.

"I'll teach him a lesson," Compton said in a nasty tone. Maybe it was because he had evil on his mind. I knew that's what it was the second I saw him pull out a knife from inside his boot top and begin walking toward the mustang. "Where I come from, you bleed these high-strung ones some, it'll take the spirit outta 'em."

He'd no sooner gotten the words out and taken all of three steps toward the mustang than Chance and I let him know where we stood. I jumped down off the corral while Chance took a couple of long strides to the man's back, grabbed him by the shoulder, and spun him around. The knife came around too, still in the man's grasp, but not for long. Chance brought his left hand down on the man's knife hand, knocking the knife loose. At the same time he brought his other hand, now formed in a fist, down across the man's face, knocking him to the ground with one blow. But like I say, both of us got into the act.

I was the only one there who hadn't taken off his gun yet, and now I had palmed mine, pointing it at Compton with the same leisurely intent I had at target practice.

"Pull that knife around here again, friend, and I'll kill you where you stand," Chance said, a hard edge to his voice that was matched only by the look on his face.

"And if he don't, I will," I added, just so the man would know we meant business.

"Gents," I continued, holstering my pistol, "in case I didn't mention it, we're in the horse-breaking business, and my brother and me are the ones you're working for here. Now, I don't give a damn if your granddaddy was a bleeder and treated his horses the same way. You hire on here and you'll do things our way or you can ride on."

"That's a fact, gentlemen," my brother said, giving the lot of them a squint that held just a bit of madness to it. "When we say breaking horses, that means you get your sorry ass up in that saddle and see how long you can outlast that horse. There'll be no cutting of meat unless it's on your plate and a meal is being served. Any questions?"

There were none.

"Good," I said after a few moments of silence. "Compton, let's see what you can do on that old hell raiser," I added, as Chance went about the process of roping and readying the mount.

Compton wasn't worth spit on a bucking mustang, but Bond and McHale did fair to middling, almost as good as Emmett, who was by far the better rider. But then he was a cavalryman. When we called it a day, I was wondering if Chance being in the cavalry was what made him a better rider than me.

I also found myself wondering if I hadn't made a mistake in my hiring process.

At least with Compton, who pretty much remained silent the rest of the day.

CHAPTER
★ 9 ★

It was the next morning that we all learned a lesson from Emmett. As it turned out, apparently he had ridden a horse or two in his career in the cavalry.

The one called Bond seemed awful anxious to make a good impression on Chance, but then no man likes being dressed down by another. Not that Chance and me knew that much about busting horses and all, you understand. It was just that we were both familiar with horses, having been raised with and introduced to them about the same time we'd found out what pistols and rifles were. Both of us realized that going off to war doesn't teach a man much more of a skill than effective killing, a profession that, for the most part, is illegal once you get back into civilian life. And since neither of us had an overwhelming desire to go on killing for a living, we decided that horses was what we knew best. We'd done some scouting around and found that ranchers in the area were always in need of good riding horses in the spring, when the roundups began and they were readying for the trail drives north, an event which had only recently begun to be a regular occurrence in Texas. Also of interest was the fact that the army was constantly in need of good riding stock. When we'd discovered that they were willing to pay upwards of twenty-five dollars for a good horse, Chance and I decided that the army was our best bet.

But like I say, Bond was anxious to prove himself that morning. He'd gulped down a serving of my pancakes and quickly disappeared before the rest of us were through with breakfast. Chance had cautioned everyone to eat a light meal, for it was quite possible they might lose it if they hit a rough ride. I made sure not to fix more than one helping for each of us, for I also knew that my brother had in mind making this a learning day for these new hired hands. The way it turned out, he actually got some learning his own self.

When we got outside, Bond was tossing a blanket and saddle on one of the mustangs in the breaking corral. We'd spent a good many hours building three different corrals, one for holding the wild mustangs, one with a stubbing post in it for our bronc breaking, and the third one for keeping the mounts we'd tamed. Bond had opened the gate and let in one of the wild mustangs, although I could see right off he'd picked a tough one.

"Damn fool," Chance muttered to himself when he saw what Bond was doing.

"Ain't that the truth," I said in agreement, shaking my head.

Most likely it was the horse that had chosen to come into the breaking corral, I thought, rather than the other way around. Mind you, he was a good strong one and all horse, but if mustang is a word you use to describe wild, well, it didn't even come close to doing it justice for this mount.

"I take it he's a tough one," Emmett said upon hearing our comments.

"Old Ass Buster," were the only three words Chance spoke, as though they said it all, and in a way they did. My brother had spent the better part of a morning last week unsuccessfully trying to get this horse saddled. The sight of Bond tossing a blanket and saddle on the horse gave Chance a look of surprise, as he added, "Damn mustang must know a pilgrim when he sees one."

Bond seemed awful confident as he calmly slipped a hackamore over the horse's muzzle and climbed aboard. At least he thought he was climbing aboard this cyclone. As he stepped into the stirrup, the horse let out a blowing sensation and Bond, saddle and all, fell to the ground. Everyone but Bond thought it was funny.

"I was right," Chance said with a smile as we climbed over the top rail and into the corral. "Old Ass Buster can spot a pilgrim just like that." He snapped his fingers.

"What are you talking about?" Bond said, his face a

deep shade of red as he slowly got to his feet, trying in vain to brush the dust from his shirt and pants.

The horse got real skittish and backed away as we neared him.

"That," Chance said, pointing toward the mustang. "Old Ass Buster knows I mean business with him and he don't like that." To Bond, he said, "He don't know you from Adam, likely figured you for a greenhorn to boot." The words were accompanied by a confident grin. Something told me my brother's main mission today was going to be making these new hands as humble as missionary monks. Horse breaking was going to be a secondary tool that he'd use to make them that way.

That was when Emmett took over as the teacher rather than the student. He stepped forward and pushed his hat back on his head some, picking up an empty grain sack hanging on the corral as he approached the mustang.

"You know, boys, it continually amazes me what you don't know about horses," he said to no one in particular, although I could have sworn I saw him give Chance and me a quick glance out of the corner of his eye. It was then I had my first inkling that this man knew more about horses than I'd given him credit for.

"Bond, get that saddle out of the way and hand me the blanket," he continued, suddenly in charge of the situation. Neither Bond, McHale, nor Compton challenged the man, and I wasn't about to tangle with a sergeant of the United States Army. I'd had enough of that kind of experience with my brother. Chance, well, I think he was picking up a certain amount of respect for the man and what he knew, his respect for the rank taking precedence over anything else, I thought. Besides, as bullheaded as my brother was, he had more sense than to stand in the way of learning something new. Like how to handle a wild mustang proper.

"You bet, Sarge," Bond said and scampered out of the way once he'd grabbed hold of the blanket and saddle and distributed them as the sergeant bade.

"You've got to let these critters know who's the boss," he said, tossing the grain sack over the horse's head, making sure it covered the animal's eyes. "Of course, you got to let him know that you trust him too." To the animal, in a much softer voice, he said, "Easy now, boy, you just play along with Emmett and we'll get along fine. Easy, now.

"Let him get a whiff of this blanket," he said in the same low voice, bringing the blanket up to the horse's nose with one hand, patting the animal on the neck with the other. "It's got the smell of horse to it and he's got to know that it ain't gonna hurt him, that I ain't gonna hurt him."

With the assurance of a knowledgeable horseman, Emmett then proceeded to rub the horse with the blanket, from neck to backside. The animal, which had been shaking with fear and standing still since it didn't trust itself to do anything without the use of its eyes, was suddenly calming down, apparently gaining confidence in the man who was now his master. This process lasted for almost ten minutes as Emmett rubbed the blanket over nearly the entire horse's body.

"There's a big difference between breaking a horse and breaking a horse's spirit," the man said once he was through.

"That's right," Chance said, trying to sound like he knew something too, I suspect. "A horse with a broken spirit ain't worth the sweat it takes to break him."

"Damn right, Chance," Emmett said. By the tone of his voice, you'd have thought he'd known my brother from somewhere in the war, when it was likely just a mutual respect for one's rank that brought them together. But who was to say? Maybe they had crossed trails during the war. You never could tell.

The horse was still blinded by the grain sack as Emmett silently continued his treatment in gaining control of this wild one. Next he placed the saddle blanket on the horse's back, then removed it, then put it back again, all the while talking soft and low to the mustang. At times I thought it a sing-songy type of talk, the kind you do with a small baby when you're trying to be gentle with it and get on its good side.

"Putting the saddle on these beasts can be a tricky thing," he said and reached for the saddle. "Sometimes you've got 'em scared enough that they'll let you put it on 'em without no problem at all. Other times it's pure fear and mad or a combination of both that makes 'em want to buck it right off." With that he tossed the saddle on the mustang as gently as possible, although I've got to tell you there isn't any real gentle way to toss a saddle on a bronc. To my surprise—and the others' as well—Old Ass Buster just stood there, still as could be.

"Where you made your mistake was tightening up

the cinch, Bond," he said, reaching under the horse's girth to grab the cinch and pull it under the animal's belly.

"How's that, Sarge?" Unlike Compton the day before, Bond seemed to have a genuine desire to learn from the man who had likely been his senior in rank if indeed he'd been in the army.

"Watch his belly," Emmett commanded, as he slipped the cinch through the o-ring on his side of the saddle. It took a careful bit of tracking to do it, but if you concentrated on it you could see the mustang take in a whole lungful of air as Emmett tried to tighten the cinch. "All right, boy, come here." From the tone of his voice, it was almost as though he were talking to one of the members of his old platoon or squad or whatever they called them in the cavalry.

Bond, a bit skittish himself now, moved closer to Emmett.

"That's why you fell on your ass, boy," he said in a snarl of disapproval. When Bond only looked confused, he added, "The goddamn horse lets out all of that air when you start to board him and there goes your riggings, not to mention you. Understand?"

"Yes, Sergeant." The young man could have still been in uniform, he sounded that terrified of this man.

"Now, how you gonna remedy that situation, son?" This was an old hand talking now.

"I don't know." At least Bond was honest in what he said, which sometimes—but not always—turned out to be the best path to follow on matters.

"Want to get rid of that excess tank of air Old Ass Buster's carrying, right?" Emmett growled, as though purely put out by talking to such ignorant people as the one next to him now.

"Yes, Sergeant."

"Remember how I told you he's gotta know that you're the boss?"

"Yes, Sergeant."

"Are you ready to ride, sonny?"

A look of pure doubt crossed the young man's face now. Still, he remembered who he was talking to when he answered with, "Yes, Sergeant. I'll try."

"Good, Bond. You make sure and hang on to your hat, 'cause I got a notion this hoss is gonna buck you so high you'll come down with Saint Peter's initials burned on your heels."

The boy tried to grin, but none of us had to guess the fear he must have been feeling at the moment.

"But Sergeant, how—"

Emmett kicked Old Ass Buster in the gut almost as hard as I'd seen Chance kick a man in his elsewheres one time. The mustang let out that same whoosh of air he had earlier, but this time Emmett was ready for him. He gave the cinch a mighty yank, tightening the cinch so much I wouldn't have been surprised if the saddle never came off that mount.

"This ain't no show-off time, boy, so when I tell you to you mount up this beast and hang on with both hands, I mean it," the sergeant said, still treating the man as though he were once one of his own. "Hold his head back as far as you can. He can't do a hell of a lot of bucking that way." Emmett's next move was similar to what Chance had done the day before. He pulled down the ear of the mustang and bit down on his ear.

Too Many Drifters

Like I said, it caused the horse to take his mind off the fact that there would soon be someone foreign on his back.

"Saddle up, Bond!" Chance said, and in an instant the man was all but jumping in the saddle.

"Let 'er rip, boy!" Emmett yelled as he released the horse's ear and pulled the grain bag from his forehead.

Suddenly Old Ass Buster recalled where he was and what his mission in life was and took to bucking as hard and far as he could. But Bond was eager to please and managed to hold his own for five or ten seconds by my rough count. He'd pulled back on the reins as hard as he could, but he hadn't quite taken command of the piece of wild meat he was riding and was soon headed for the ground.

"Roll, boy! Roll! Roll! Roll!" Emmett yelled as Bond hit the dirt in what can only be described as a spread-eagle position. He must have heard the sergeant's yell too, for it was as he looked over his shoulder and saw Old Ass Buster rearing up to come down on top of him that he took the sergeant's advice real quick. If he hadn't, he wouldn't have lasted out the day.

Chance was off the top rail as quick as could be, snatching up the rope to the hackamore and tying it around the snubbing post, firmly planting his feet in the dirt and standing fast. By the time the horse had calmed down, Emmett had helped Bond to his feet and was guiding him to our side of the corral.

"Not bad for a beginner, son, not bad," Emmett said, slapping the young man heartily on the back.

"Thank you, Sergeant," Bond choked, clearing

some dust from his throat. He didn't have to say anymore than that, for I knew he'd just received high praise from the noncom next to him.

"You know, boys, having brains ain't a requirement to do this kind of work," Emmett said, taking us all in as he spoke. "But you damn sure better have guts." He looked at Bond and gave him a wink and a nod. "You've got guts, Bond, I'll give you that. Yes, sir." High praise, indeed.

"Who's next?" Chance said.

"Let's see if this old hoss remembers me," Emmett said and strolled toward the mustang. "What do you say, old boy?" Chance held tight on his rein as Emmett closed in on Old Ass Buster.

I don't know if he thought he was being sneaky when he casually reached down and picked up the grain bag again, but the horse didn't seem to mind or didn't care, one. All he seemed to notice was the low, soft voice of the man beside him now who was also treating him with a bit of kindness. I had a notion Emmett was having second thoughts about tossing that grain bag over the mustang's face, but he finally did it, mostly as a precautionary movement, I reckon. Then, still talking low, he patted the horse lightly on the neck and moved back to its side. Chance had loosened the rein from the snubbing post and moved around to the front of the mustang now, ready to pull off the grain bag whenever Emmett told him. He transferred the reins to Emmett, who then stuck a foot in a stirrup and was halfway aboard this cyclone when he said, "Now!"

Chance pulled off the bag and got the hell out of the

way as the mustang tried once again to see if he could kick Saint Peter in the teeth with his hind feet. But Emmett was a good rider—the best I'd seen at this game, in fact. If there is such a thing as rolling with the punches, Emmett did it with Old Ass Buster. The animal frog hopped, came down stiff-legged, turned a hundred and eighty degrees in the air as he did, but still didn't buck Emmett out of the saddle. It must have seemed like an eternity but couldn't have been more than a minute or so that the two opponents went at it with one another. The sergeant was a tough one, though, and he managed to stay atop Old Ass Buster despite the hellacious ride. Suddenly the horse was spirited although not wholly wild, as I'd seen him before. He pranced around the corral as though he owned the place now. Or maybe it was Emmett who owned the place.

"You go up and fork a cloud like this mustang just had me doing, and you might not bust anything, but you damn sure do get the hinges and bolts loosened up," he said with a smile when he stopped by us. "Rope you a hoss, Wash, and let's take us a ride," Emmett said, and I was inclined to agree.

I dragged my saddle blanket and saddle over to the third corral, where we kept the two or three horses that we'd broken so far and picked out one that had a lot of run left in him. He'd gotten used to the saddle and blanket, mind you, but he was still frisky as could be and liked running.

Chance assured us that he could handle everything on this end of the operation, which I didn't doubt at all. Like I say, he's fast to pick up on useful operations, and this was one of them. I figured that McHale and Compton would have dusted their britches by the time we got back from running these mounts.

And run we did. It was a good thing too, for Old Ass Buster had a lot of run left in him, just like Emmett said. We circled a bit north, then headed west, then turned south, as I led Emmett to the box canyon Chance and I had discovered and decided to use. It was also down in this area that we'd come across several wild horse herds, one of them from which we'd captured the very mustangs we now had in our possession.

"It's amazing what you can come across in this country," I said when we came to a stop not far from the box canyon. We'd both had a good ride and it seemed a good place to stop for the moment.

"I believe you," Emmett said, taking in the countryside we'd been traveling through. "I hear old Jim Bowie left a lost silver mine somewhere hereabouts. Be a nice piece of change if we could dig up that piece of treasure."

"Yeah"—I laughed—"but most folks around here doubt that it even exists, if it ever was."

"Still . . ."

"Yeah." I smiled at the man, knowing greed when I see it and knowing the thoughts that were going through his mind just then. They were the same ones that had gone through my own mind years and years ago in my youth, thoughts that were long since gone.

"There's a box canyon over there," I continued, pointing to an area not a mile from us. "Chance and me put in a helluva lot of time and effort to put a swinging gate up that we could use to trap some wild horses when we wanted."

"Interesting," was all Emmett said. Then, squinting as though looking at something far away, he added, "Looks like you got some fellas making a dry camp up there. Keeping an eye on it for you, are they?"

"No," I replied and squinted my own self at the entrance to the canyon. I'd been so taken by the horses and the riding that I'd missed what was suddenly the obvious: half a dozen men and their horses right where Emmett had pointed them out. "Don't look like anybody I know."

The sergeant's hands went down to his side and he suddenly realized that he had no weaponry on him. I was pulling my rifle out of its boot by the time he said, "Got an extra weapon?"

"Here," I said, checking the Colt revolving rifle I carried in my rifle boot. It was a good rifle, although it had its faults. Sort of like a lot of men, I reckon. I tossed it to Emmett.

"Thanks."

Without so much as a discussion, we were on our way to the camp at the box canyon. In less than two minutes we were upon the campsite.

"This is your country, Wash," Emmett said when we reined in before the group of men who were now numbering seven or so. Between what they were carrying on their mounts and wearing on their hips, I'd say they were pretty well armed. Kelly's Hardware could do a lot of business with these fellows, I thought. "You know any of these birds?"

"Nope," I said, giving the bunch a look over. I'd say

they had been traveling for some time, for none looked like they'd been near a sharp-edged razor for at least a week. "Passing through, are you?"

"Yeah," one said in a frown. "What's it to you? Free country, ain't it?"

"That's what I understand," I said with a shrug. "I just like knowing who my neighbors are."

"Like he said, just passing through," another hardcase said.

"Bully for you, son," Emmett said, his voice having as much of a snarl as it had earlier when he'd shown Bond how to right a wild mustang. "Just make sure you keep on moving."

"Do you keep him on a leash or what?" the first one said in a smart-alecky tone.

"Fact of the matter is I do," I said. "Better watch out or I'll turn him loose on you. He ain't been fed today yet, you know."

"Smart ass," another growled.

Emmett had been carrying the Colt rifle in the crook of his arm, but in the breath of a second it was pointed at the man who had just run off at the mouth.

"I'm about to kill you, sonny," he said without so much as a twinge in his voice. "Yes sir . . ."

"Why don't you let him live, Emmett," I said. "I ain't really up to burying anyone just now. Besides, we oughtta be getting back to the ranch."

"I don't know, I still got the urge—"

"Better listen to your friend, mister," the leader of the bunch said. "You ain't got a chance in hell of getting out of this alive."

"My, but ain't you a feisty one today," Emmett said with a taunting smile. He was just waiting for one of them to make a false move, just waiting for a reason to kill one of them. I was beginning to understand why he had made sergeant so often. He seemed to search out trouble as much as Pardee Taylor. Emmett switched the point of aim of his Colt from one loudmouth to another. "Has it crossed your mind that even if I die at the hands of your amigos, you ain't gonna be around to celebrate it? Are you really that stupid?"

"Emmett?" The man grunted something to me, still paying attention to the man he had his rifle trained on. "Remember what I said? The burying and all?"

I knew these pilgrims had fighting on their mind, so by the time they turned to me, I had my LeMat in my hands, ready to put a slug in the first one to make a move.

"Gentlemen, I'd appreciate it if you were off this piece of land within twenty-four hours," I said in my most accommodating tone. "I'll be back then."

"I thought this was a free country," the leader said.

"Oh, it is, mister. But I was here first. Now how about undoing those gunbelts," I added with a bit of a snarl. "I never did get used to being back shot." I smiled and added, "It's not that I don't trust you. I just don't trust you. If you know what I mean."

"Believe me, Wash," Emmett said, looking over his shoulder as we left, "they know what you mean."

I do believe they did.

CHAPTER
★ 10 ★

It wasn't until the evening meal that night that I made mention of the run-in Emmett and I had with the strangers over by the area we were calling Horse Trap Canyon. For the most part it seemed to pass as just one more incident in a day filled with many other notable events. The events, of course, were the attempts by Bond, McHale, and Compton to fork a bronc and see how long they could stay on. Sore? To hear them talk, it didn't even come close to describing how they felt.

"Let me tell you, Mr. Carston," Compton said to me over his meal, "I felt so crippled by the time we called it a day, why, all you'd have had to do was give me a fistful of lead pencils and it would be complete."

Too Many Drifters

I thought I saw a hint of a smile as the man spoke. At least he was making an effort to get along now.

"I'll tell you what, Compton," I said between bites of my own meal, "if you promise not to try bleeding our mustangs, you might as well call me Wash." I shrugged. "Everybody else does. Besides, I'm not that formal." Hell, somebody had to try to make friends with the man.

That trace of a grin began to grow some as the man looked at me and replied, "You've got a deal." No handshake was needed to seal it, just a nod of the head. It's the way things are done out here. Besides, no one likes being interrupted during meal eating. Just ask Chance.

One thing about being in a war, you meet one hell of a lot of people. Most of them are from all different walks of life, so if you're smart and pay attention you'll pick up a lot about those people, both individually and as a whole. It's a real education, and a smart man will make the most of it. Me, I'd seen a lot of men like Compton during my time with the Confederacy. It wasn't that they were always young and misguided, you understand, for that wasn't the case. I'd say it was being unwanted that hurt the most. Hell, I'd felt that way my own self when I'd left home to join the C.S.A. Me and Pa had gone through a real fandango about signing up with the Rebs, and I was just young enough and hardheaded enough to take off on my own once he'd gotten through chewing me up one side and down the other. I'd never asked Chance how it was when he'd left to join the Union forces, but knowing my brother and my father, it was likely about the same as when I left. I'd been getting the notion that Compton was that kind of person, one who'd spent a lot of his time in the service alone and not belonging to anyone, maybe not even his own unit. No man should have to feel that way.

"Think you'll stay in this country long?" I asked when supper was over and we'd gone outside to watch the sun set. Any other day we would likely be working from can see to can't see, but these fellows had done a pretty good day's work, according to Chance, so between us we decided to knock off early today.

"I don't know, this is a big country," was Compton's reply in a much friendlier tone. "Maybe I'll see how much I can take in before I think about settling down."

"A lot of men seem to be doing that," I said, taking a sip of what would be my last cup of coffee of the day. "My pa keeps telling me and my brother stories about places he's been and things he's done. Seems to me like you could go on forever out here and never see it all."

I knew that getting too abrupt with a man like this could make him skittish, scare him away as easily as one of those wild horses we were trying to cultivate. But then humans are a lot different from wild mustangs for the most part, needing a lot of currying and soft talk to get to know them. Jump on one like you would a horse like Old Ass Buster and you'd lose him right quick. I reckon it's the nature of the beast.

The six of us went through a bit of small talk that night, most of it about the bronc twisting we'd be doing the next day, but called it an early night. Time was too precious to waste out here, so we all knew

Too Many Drifters

Chance and me planned for all of us to be at those corrals at the crack of dawn. No time to burn daylight, especially where making money was concerned. And these horses were money in the bank.

It was three hours past sunup the next day that we had some visitors. I could see their dust long before I could hear them, and it made me take caution for it looked to be upwards of half a dozen of them.

"Chance, we got company, but I ain't sure whether it's social or trouble," I said when I first pointed the dust out to him.

"How so?" he asked. McHale had just got his shirt dirty again on another tough ride and my brother told Compton to get the rider out of the way of the mustang before turning his attention back to me. Once Chance was at my side, I had everyone's attention as well.

"You think it's them birds we run into yesterday?" Emmett said, climbing up on the top rail, as though taking a place on what we were calling the opry seat would give him a better look at them.

"If it's them and they're as mean as you say, I've a notion they ain't gonna be sociable atall," Chance said. To our new hands, he said, "Boys, let's take us a break from all this hard work and ready us for some target practice. If you know what I mean."

McHale smiled at my brother. "Know exactly what you mean, boss."

By the time they got within sight, we were armed to the teeth. Trouble was we didn't really need to be. Turned out the half dozen riders were wearing Union uniforms. Mind you, that could have been trouble too, the way some Union forces thought they were almighty God since this war was over, but these were some men from the army we knew, although briefly.

"How are you Carston boys doing?" the young lieutenant said, giving us an offhand salute as he rode up.

"Not bad, Lieutenant," Chance said with a cordial smile. "How about you and your men?" It was a good thing my brother had decided to do the talking, for I had a distinct aversion to being called a boy by a young man who wasn't any older than me.

"Fine, just fine." The officer looked about and saw the horses in the corrals. "We were patrolling the area and thought we'd stop by and see how you're doing with those mounts you're breaking for us."

"There's seven of 'em in that furthest corral, Lieutenant," Chance said, pointing out the horses. "They're pretty much saddle broke and used to a man on 'em now. What they need is a good ride now and then to get any more question they have about who's the boss out of 'em."

"I can use them right now, if you're willing to release them," the man said.

I reckon a gleam came into all of our eyes about then. Like I said, these broncs meant money.

"What do you think, Wash?" Chance said to me, more to show me that he was consulting me than anything else, I thought. Chance is good at shoving it down your throat if he knows good and damn well he's right and you're wrong.

"You got a deal, mister," I said to the lieutenant.

"At the agreed-upon price?" my brother threw in, as

the officer dismounted and searched about his saddlebags for the tools necessary to complete the deal.

"Of course," he replied. "Twenty-five dollars a head, wasn't it?"

"That's right," Chance said, although I noticed him getting a mite nervous, and with good reason.

I pulled him off to the side, guiding him by the elbow out of hearing distance of the others.

"I thought you told me it was twenty dollars a head," I said, a distinctive frown forming on my forehead.

"A minor detail, brother," Chance said, even more nervous now. Still, he was strong enough to get out of my grip as he said, "We'll discuss it later." Then he was back with the group of men, watching over the lieutenant as the man did his figuring and writing.

I knew Lieutenant Forbush was authorized to sign for these horses and that he could pay us on the spot if need be. And twenty-five dollars was a fine piece of change for seven mounts, coming to a hundred and seventy-five dollars if my figuring was right. I was just experiencing a prime case of how my brother must have been feeling when I told him I'd closed out our account and moved it to another bank. Besides, I hate being lied to.

"Emmett, why don't you and the boys give the lieutenant and his men a hand," Chance said. To the officer, he said, "If you've got some decent riders, maybe you'd like to saddle up and have them ride the mounts back to your post."

"Sounds like a good idea. Sergeant, let's do just that," he said to the senior NCO with him.

"This way, lads," Emmett said, leading the group to the corral. "Let's just hope we ain't rid the new off of 'em yet."

Everyone had gone except Lieutenant Forbush when Chance turned to me with a sheepish smile.

"Now then, little brother, about those horses . . ."

I hit him hard, right across the jaw. Not once but twice. First with my right and then with my left. I don't mind telling you that it hurt my fists something fierce doing it, but it sure felt good. Compensation, I reckon you'd say, for the five-dollar difference in price. I stunned my brother with those blows, sending him reeling backward before he knew what had hit him. I didn't stop then, just stepped forward and moved in on him again, hitting him twice more with as many fists until he dropped on his ass in a sitting position. Pa keeps saying that being mad will get more done for you than anything else. I reckon he's right, for I was awful goddamn mad.

"Is there something wrong with the deal?" the lieutenant asked, likely as stunned as Chance.

Like I said, I was mad. "Nothing really, Lieutenant. Just a minor detail that needed to be taken care of," I growled at him.

"Is there something I should—"

"What you should do, *sonny,* is get your horses and your men and git outta here before I decide to take you out of that saddle and make you a part of what I'm doing to him," I said, hoping the fool caught on to the pure meanness I was feeling. "I ain't in a real sociable mood at the moment."

"Are you sure—"

"It really ain't none of your goddamn business,

sonny," I growled again. To hell with this lieutenant and calling me a boy.

"I'd listen to him, son," Emmett said, seeing Chance still sitting there, still rubbing his jaw, still wondering what was going on. "He's one of the honchos here, you know."

The lieutenant gave a confused look in my brother's direction. "But does he—"

"Now, son, I don't know as I can give you the particulars, but I'd say he knows," Emmett said with a sly grin. "Oh yeah, he knows."

CHAPTER
★ 11 ★

Emmett made it a point not to ask what was going on between Chance and me once the lieutenant and his men were gone with their horses. He made it a bigger point to keep his three compadres from making any similar inquiries. I reckon they all had in mind the words Chance and I had spoken to them, the ones about being paid whenever we got our money for the horses.

"You know, hoss, you look like you could use a drink," Emmett said as he offered Chance a hand and got my brother back on his feet.

"I'd bet a dollar you know just where to get one too," Chance said, knowing full well what the sergeant was getting around to.

Too Many Drifters

Emmett produced an immediate smile, which broadened considerably as he said, "You'd win your bet too, hoss."

I rubbed my jaw in thought. "Gee, I don't know, fellas. Now, McHale here, why he's bit the dust already a couple of times this morning. I might consider letting him cut the dust some over to Ernie Johnson's, but . . ."

"Oh, but them mustangs took a heap of doing to saddle and all, and them soldier boys wasn't no help, you know," Emmett said, acting all tuckered out. He even ran a forearm across his brow to show how hard he'd been working. Trouble was it didn't produce any sweat on the sleeve.

"And your tonsils got dusted something fierce and need washing off, right?" I said. The whole thing was reminiscent of the way we tried to cajole Pa into this, that, and the other back when we were youngsters.

"You betcha, boss," the big sergeant agreed in a hearty voice.

"What do you think, brother?" I said to Chance, although I was careful to maintain my distance from the man.

Chance was rubbing his jaw, although we all knew it had nothing to do with the thought process.

"Well, I likely could use a drink," he admitted. "But I'd wager we got at least another hour before old Ernie opens that jug juice palace of his. Ary you boys are willing to polish your britches on a couple more of these broncs, I reckon we can call it an early day today."

That got approval all around and we spent the next hour and some seeing who could stay in the saddle longest. Not that it was any kind of contest, you understand. I reckon it just helped pass the time in a way. It sure made it a hell of a lot more interesting. One thing I made sure and take note of was how all three of them—Bond, McHale, and Compton—were catching on to the orders that Chance and Emmett were barking out to them. It was almost as though the two exsergeants had taken over joint command of the operation. Me, I fit in where I could, even doing some riding.

According to my pocket watch, it was just after eleven when we got into Twin Rifles that morning. We'd stayed on the last bronc a mite longer than we'd planned to but made sure we had him good and ready for the corral by the time we were through with him. Given a chance, I imagine our new hands would have changed clothes and put on some new duds before coming into town to celebrate, but they had none to begin with, so we just cleaned up as best we could and made our way into town.

"You boys tell Ernie to give you a drink on me," Chance said as we all dismounted in front of the saloon. "Me and Wash got to go to the bank and cash this check. We'll have you some pay directly." Emmett led the rest into the saloon as Chance and me headed for Phineas McDougal's new bank. "Besides," my brother said in an offhand way, giving me a hard look, "I want to see this new bank my money's in. Maybe they've finished it by now, huh?"

The inside of the Surety Savings and Loan Bank looked a lot more businesslike than the first time I'd been in it a few days back. The smell of paint permeated the area and the inside had a much more civilized appearance to it, as though it was just the place to bring your money for investment. Or maybe those are the wrong words. I reckon it just looked more inviting to the human eye. More trusting, if you will.

"I seen gambling houses painted up just as pretty as this," Chance said as we walked in.

"Why do you say that?" I asked, not understanding his comment at first.

A crooked smile came across my brother's face as he added, "They took your money too."

"True," I agreed, "but they didn't keep it."

Chance's face became more serious now. "Damn right," he said with a firm nod of the head. "I won it back." There are some things with my brother you just can't win, and they include passionate arguments. The man is determined to have the last word. I let this conversation end right there.

The lieutenant had made the check out to both of us so it took both our signatures to cash it. I suggested that we put a hundred dollars in the account and use the rest to pay off our new bronc busters and a couple of bills we'd run up in town. I particularly wanted to pay off the amount we'd run up in the general store. Flour and coffee don't come cheap, you know.

"What about Emmett and the boys?" Chance said. "What did you have in mind paying them?"

"Looks to me like they're working out," I said. "How about five or ten dollars each? At Ernie's prices, they should be able to drink the place dry if they try hard."

Chance gave me a disgruntled grin. "Yeah, five dollars for a couple days' work ain't too bad, I reckon."

We were walking out of the bank, fixing on heading for Ernie Johnson's saloon to pay our riders, when the batwing doors of the saloon flew open and out came Pardee Taylor. He wasn't walking either. Not even what looked like a stroll. No sir. Rolling out was more like it. Ass over elbow onto the boardwalk and down onto the dirty main street. Our new riders had taken easier falls than the one I'd just seen Pardee take.

By the time Pardee was sprawled out on the street, Emmett was standing on the boardwalk in front of the saloon. Hands on hips, a stern look about him, it was plain to see Pardee had been tangling with the wrong man again. He seemed to be doing a lot of that lately.

"This boy just don't know the value of getting a free beer once in a while," Emmett said in what can only be described as a disappointed fatherly voice. I only needed to hear his comment to figure out that John Fitch was in the saloon, likely buying a drink or two for Emmett and his friends. Once I'd fit that into place, the rest came pretty easily.

"Pardee still name calling John?" Chance said.

Emmett nodded. To Pardee Taylor, he said, "I never was much of a preaching man, son, but in your case I think it's time I made an exception."

Pardee was on his feet now, angry as could be from the look of him. "We'll see about that," he said and took no more than three big steps toward Emmett before he was met by one of the sergeant's big fists, which landed a blow across his face that sent him reeling backward again, falling flat on his git-up end.

"You take a swing at me again, sonny, and they'll carry you out of this town," Emmett said and took a step down off the boardwalk onto the dirt street.

"You seem to be a hateful son of a bitch," he continued, now totally in control of the situation. "Well, I'm gonna tell you something and I want you to listen, Mr. Pardee Taylor.

"The next time you get the urge to tell a man to go back where he come from, I want you to think back real hard. Now, *if* you can do that, and *if* your brain isn't so taken with whiskey it can't understand a thing going on inside you, I want you to think back on where it is *you* come from.

"You see, boy, when you start telling people to go back where they come from, why, you might's well pack your own things and head on out too. Hell, sonny, *Everybody* comes from somewhere!"

"Yeah? I come from right here in Texas," Pardee said belligerently.

Emmett just shook his head the way a teacher will when confronted by a student who is harder than usual to teach. "Want to do this the hard way, huh?" I heard the man mumble to himself under his breath.

"Let me ask you something, sonny," Emmett continued, not giving Pardee a chance to think or respond anymore than he already had. "Where'd your daddy come from? Or your mama? Any idea?"

Pardee shrugged in silence, deep in thought it seemed, before saying, "England, I reckon. I ain't sure."

"Well, if you ain't for sure about where you come from your own self, how in the hell can you stand there and tell a man to go back to where he come from? Damn but that's stupid," Emmett said, his own mad stirred up now.

"I can say anything I want to!" was Pardee's reply.

"Oh, sure you can," Emmett agreed. "And you can die anywhere in this land too. Of course, you ain't always gonna get to choose where, but you'll only do it once. I guarantee you that."

"I reckon what the man's saying, Pardee," I said, finally picking up on Emmett's line of thought, "is that we're all related to immigrants in one way or another. If our daddies didn't come from some foreign land, then our granddaddies did."

"Wash is right," I heard Pa say over my shoulder. "Why, I read somewhere that even the Indians out here come from a far-away land they call Siberia. God only knows where it's located at, but it ain't anywhere close to this part of Texas, that's for sure."

"You just mind your manners and stop being so goddamn hateful," Emmett said, still standing there with his hands on his hips, ready to take Pardee on, any time, any how. He must have figured he'd had the last word on the subject, for his next move was to give Chance and me a look and say, "Now then, if my employers have got my pay for me, I'll buy you a drink, sonny."

"You would?" Pardee was as stunned as the rest of us, I reckon.

"You just belly up to the bar in there and have the bar man pour you a drink," Emmett said, the authority of an NCO clearly present in the man. Pardee

Too Many Drifters

Taylor wasn't one to pass up a drink anymore than Chance will pass up a free meal, so he started laying tracks toward the batwing doors. But just as he reached them, Emmett said, "Oh, and son?"

"Yes, sir." All of a sudden Pardee had manners—a minor miracle, you'd think.

"Why don't you tell old John Fitch how sorry you are for making such an ass of yourself these last couple of days."

The red started to creep up Pardee's neck as he humbly said, "Yes, sir."

"Well, I'll be damned," Chance muttered to himself in amazement.

"Are you sure you want to give that man a drink?" I asked, not sure that what Emmett was doing was entirely sane.

"Why hell, Wash, I had a lot worse knuckleheads under my command when I was in the army," the sergeant said with a grin. Then, eyeing Chance, he added, "Some of 'em even went on to make sergeant. That boy just needed a mite of straightening out."

"Along with a manners lesson," Chance said with the same amount of grin showing.

I gauged that the two men definitely understood one another, if their looks meant anything. "Yeah, that too," Emmett said in agreement.

"Here," Chance said, plunking a fistful of gold coins down in Emmett's hand. "I'm making you the finance officer for those yahoos in there. Wash and me figure you got ten dollars coming for helping out with the bronc twisting the way you have. I may even admit to having learned a thing or two. The other three get five dollars each."

"The more horses we break the quicker we'll make the money and the more there'll be," I added.

"Sounds fair, friend," Emmett said. Then, pocketing the coins, he placed a brotherly arm around each of us and led us into Ernie Johnson's saloon. "Come on, boys, I'll buy you each a drink."

CHAPTER
★ 12 ★

I only had one drink but, as I'd suspected, Emmett and his friends tried to drink the place dry on their skimpy pay. But then at a quarter a drink for the hard stuff, it wasn't hard to get fairly drunk before your money ran out. Which was just what the four of them managed to do before the evening meal came around.

Chance stayed at Ernie Johnson's a mite longer than I did but had the good sense to leave before he'd gotten a bellyful of rotgut. Me, I spent some time making the rounds of the general store and a few others in town we'd run up bills at and paid most of them off. Hell, somebody had to manage the money on our place.

It was later that afternoon that Chance and I helped

Pa guide Pardee Taylor, Emmett, and his friends into the hoosegow. They were all drunker than a lord and philosophical as could be. Emmett recognized me and, through some kind of gibberish I'm sure he thought to be quite lucid, tried telling me that Pardee Taylor wasn't such a bad guy after all. I tried to keep a straight face, remembering the hell-for-leather attitude the sergeant had taken with the man earlier in the day, while Chance just laughed himself silly at the thought of Pardee Taylor as a friendly sort. No sooner were the drunks seated in their cells than they all fell asleep, either laying against one another or passing out and rolling off onto the floor. I reckon Pa's slept on too many hard floors in his time to think any man should have to sleep in such a position and was soon sorting them out so each man had at least a bunk to sleep the night away in.

It must have been a little after four that afternoon when a rider came galloping down the street as fast as the wind. Chance and me were still in Pa's office, contemplating what to do with our drunken riders and where to eat our supper meal, when we heard the clip clop of a fast-moving horse. We each glanced out the window, then at one another.

"Joshua?" we both said in unison.

"Yup," Pa confirmed. "It's about time." I'd clean forgotten that Pa's deputy was due back from his trip to ferret out information on Phineas McDougal, our new banker. For that matter, I'd pretty much forgotten about Phineas McDougal.

Not ten minutes later Joshua came rushing through the door to the jail, as winded as that mount he'd ridden in on.

"Here you go, Joshua," Pa said and shoved a hot cup of coffee in his deputy's hand. Joshua took the cup and a grateful sip, plunking himself down in a chair next to Pa's desk. None of us was going to say anything about where he'd been for the ten minutes since riding down the city streets, for we all knew that any good rider would tend to his horse first once the ride was through, and Joshua was no exception.

"I tell you, Will, that hoss is gonna need one awful lot of rest," he said. "Not to mention a couple of good feedings."

"You look like you could use a good feeding too," Pa said, taking in the man's already gaunt features.

"Yeah, but listen, Will, have I got a lowdown to tell you about old Phineas what's-his-name," he started to say, catching his breath.

Pa held a finger to his mouth for silence, then glanced over his deputy's shoulder at the cells to the rear of the room. The drunks seemed awful quiet, but you never could tell.

"Joshua, it's getting to be about eating time and me and the boys are going over to the Porter Cafe for supper," Pa said. "Ary we get there before everyone else, why, I do believe we can find us a table off to the side so you can fill us in on old Phineas."

"Well now, Will, that's the best offer I've had today," Joshua said with a smile, setting his coffee cup down and sloshing on his hat once more.

"That's right," Chance added, with what he must have thought to be a wry smile but was actually a leer. "And Wash ain't had an opportunity to take a gander at Sarah Ann of late either."

"Don't start, Chance," Pa said as we headed for the

door, "or I'll tell her to cut your ration of food." That seemed to shut my brother right up.

"Now then, Joshua, what's all the fuss about?" Pa said once Sarah Ann had brought coffee for all of us and taken our orders.

"It's like this, Will," Joshua said and, lowering his voice, filled us in on what he'd found out.

Phineas McDougal might have been his name, it seems, but he'd known the inside of a jail on more than one occasion. These occasions had nothing to do with disorderly conduct or drunkenness, like Emmett and his boys. Oh, he hadn't killed anyone, which seemed harmless enough in a way, but what he had been involved in wasn't what you look for in most honest men.

"What do you think, Will?" Joshua asked as Sarah Ann began setting down our plates of beef and potatoes and biscuits.

We fell suddenly quiet, although it was as much because there was hot food on the table as the fact that we didn't want anyone outside the four of us to hear this conversation. Most of the next fifteen minutes was spent eating our food. When someone else can prepare it for you, there just never seems to be time to do anything but finish off that food.

"What's the matter, Wash?" Pa asked when he was through with his meal. "You look worried."

I didn't realize it but I did have a sour look on my face now. It wasn't that I didn't know what it was for either. I did. It had happened about halfway through the meal, when I'd looked out the window and seen what looked like half a dozen men riding into town. It was the fact that I recognized them that made me a mite squeamish and made me lose the taste for my food.

"Remember I was telling you about those yahoos Emmett and me come across the other day out by Horse Trap Canyon?" I said.

Pa and Chance nodded, remembering the incident, I thought.

"Well, I think I just seen 'em ride into town, only one of them was missing." A cold feeling ran through me and I felt a sudden chill run down my spine, although I thought I knew the reason for it.

"Know what you mean, son," Pa said. "That's been bothering me too."

"What's that?" Chance asked.

"Drifters. We get a new bank opened up and right away I'm seeing more drifters come into and leave this town than I do in a whole year's worth of time. There's just too damn many drifters."

"Forget about that, Will," Joshua said impatiently. "I asked you before, what are you gonna do about Phineas what's-his-name?"

"I reckon I'll check him out tomorrow morning," Pa said with what must have been infinite patience. "The banks are closed now, you know."

"What about the drifters?" Chance asked, finishing off his coffee.

"Those fellas I can do something about."

"What's that, Pa?" I asked.

Pa pushed himself away from the table and stood at his full height, placing his hat squarely on his head as he prepared to leave.

"I'm gonna park my git-up end in a chair across

from Ernie Johnson's saloon and make sure those birds leave town before the sun sets." Pa took a couple of steps toward the door, then stopped, looking back at us. "Chance, Wash, why don't you stay the night over at Miss Margaret's. You'll have to take your new hands back with you tomorrow morning anyway."

"Any other reason to stay the night?" I asked.

"Yeah. I want you with me and Joshua when we see Mr. McDougal tomorrow morning as his bank opens."

The drifters left in a peaceable fashion that night so Pa didn't have to put himself out over them. Chance and I slept at the Ferris House, run by Margaret Ferris. Margaret and her daughter made us breakfast and we were joined by Pa and Joshua. It had to be one of the longest breakfast meals I've ever eaten, for we were served at sunrise and must have sat there at the community table for a good two hours afterward.

"We could have busted a couple of them broncs by now," Chance said about eight o'clock.

"Not the way Emmett and his boys must be feeling," I said with a grin. "Unless you figure it's just the two of us doing the riding." It was easy to see that the thought pained my older brother and I said no more about it.

"Let's go," Pa finally said around quarter to nine, and we made our way to the newly established Surety Savings and Loan Bank.

It looked awful quiet as we approached the bank, but then most banks do look that way before they open. For some unknown reason, the people in those institutions move around like some kind of mouse sneaking away a piece of cheese to his hole.

Pa tried the door, but it was locked. "Mr. McDougal, are you there?" he then asked, knocking on the door.

"I'm gonna check the side," Chance said, but I noticed he had pulled his gun and did the same as Pa, following him around the building. "Door's locked," Chance said after giving the side door a good turn and a shake.

"You ever try picking a lock, Chance?" I asked.

"No. There's a faster way," he said and held his pistol up to the padlock, giving me only enough time to back out of the way before he shot the lock off the door.

He was in the bank in an instant, and I was not far behind him. If we were expecting to be greeted by thieves we needn't have worried.

The bank was empty.

"The people of this town must have had twenty thousand dollars in this bank," I said, suddenly struck with awe at how much money there was in this town.

"And you were foolish enough to be one of them to put your money in this damned place," Chance said, mad as could be.

I felt guilty as a fool could under the circumstances.

"I reckon Joshua was right last night," I said in a less than humble voice.

"Yeah," Chance said with a growl, "our Phineas McDougal is a confidence man."

CHAPTER
★ 13 ★

A half dozen citizens were standing out front when Chance and I opened the door to the bank. By the looks of them, they weren't in any too festive a mood, especially if Pa had already explained to them our suspicions.

"How much did they take, young man?" an old biddy whose name I couldn't remember asked. I'd always thought of her as the town gossip more than anything.

"Everything, ma'am," Chance replied in as cordial a voice as possible. It was a real effort for my brother, since he and I also had our money in this bank. I felt lucky he wasn't shoving the fact down my throat right now. When Chance is right, he don't let go. "Cleaned out the safe and every bit of paper money and gold coin there was."

A gasp went up among the bank customers, as though they all shared the same feelings. The next thing to happen was a goodly amount of whispered gossip between them as they exchanged glances and finally turned their gaze on the town marshal.

"What do you intend to do about it, Marshal?" the town gossip demanded.

"Why, get it back, of course!" Pa said in a tone nearly as full of frustration as the people he was conversing with. "That's a stupid question," he added, looking directly at the scowling face of the old woman who'd originally made the demand. I had the distinct notion that if he hurt her feelings he didn't really care. Hell, she'd hurt his enough with her sharp words, and you just don't do that to Pa and get away with it.

"Don't you folks worry," I said, somehow feeling it was time I did some reassuring of my own. "We'll get the town's money back for you, every last red cent. We'll be forming a posse to go after 'em in no time at all." I wished the words had conjured up more hope for the people I was talking to, but I knew they didn't, not by the looks on their faces. They'd lost their entire life's savings overnight and there wasn't a damn thing that could be done about it was what they were likely thinking.

"Good Lord, Will, what's going on?" Joshua asked back at the jail. He was outside watching what looked to be a flurry of activity as people were going quickly from one store to another, probably spreading word of the bank robbery. "Black Plague set in, did it?"

"It might as well have," Pa said with a grunt and headed inside, grabbing a cup and pouring coffee for himself and anyone else who wanted some. Seeing Emmett and his boys sitting around like they owned the place and drinking his coffee didn't help his disposition any. "And what are you three doing?"

"I reckon that's my fault, Will," Joshua said with a sheepish grin. "I give 'em some of the hot stuff with a mite of the hair of the dog. You know how it is."

"Lucky I don't charge you for it," was all Pa could mutter. Then he was suddenly silent, his mind caught up in thought.

"You want to get a posse going, Pa?" Chance asked, making his way to the rifle rack and grabbing up a handful of the long guns.

"Put 'em back," Pa said with a frown. Chance looked at me, then back at Pa in a look of shock. I found myself sporting the same questioning look my brother had on his face.

"What was that, Pa?" I asked in awe. It was the first time I'd ever heard Pa tell either one of us to replace a rifle in his rack when there was trouble about. The very first time!

"A posse? What are you fellers yammering about?" Joshua asked. With a chuckle, he added, "Somebody rob a bank or something?"

"As a matter of fact that's exactly what happened." Pa said in a stiff tone of voice. I reckon admitting to something like that in your own town is kind of hard.

"What!"

"It's that goddamn carpetbagger," Chance added by way of explanation.

Too Many Drifters

"Why that scoundrel! I knew he wasn't worth two cents," Joshua said with a shake of his finger.

"Well, he's worth a helluva lot more now," I said, the anger growing from my own feeling of loss. "What I want to know is, what are you keeping those rifles in that rack for, Pa? You ain't done nothing like that before."

"'Cause I ain't going, son."

Chance looked at me silently before turning his attention to Pa. "What did you say?" He couldn't believe his ears anymore than I could.

"But Will, that's a part of—"

"I ain't gonna say I told you so, boys, but I told you so," Pa said with a straight face. At least he was civil about it when he shoved it down our throats. I was about to mention to him that it was his job to take care of things like this but didn't get the chance anymore than Joshua had. "Raise your hands, boys," he said.

"Huh?"

"Git 'em up or I'll pull this Remington and get 'em up the other way," Pa now demanded.

Chance and I simply gave one another strange looks and did as the man bade.

"Now then, by the power vested in me by the State of Texas and these here United States, I hereby appoint you two temporary deputy U.S. marshals. Pay's a dollar a day." Then, letting out a tank full of air, he sighed and said, "That does it. Just to make it legal, you understand."

"But Pa—"

"Look, boys, I got a certain responsibility to the

people of this town—namely, protecting 'em. And this town marshal's badge don't go no further than the city limits of this town. Besides, I got bigger fish to fry."

"Bigger fish—"

"None of your damn business," Pa growled, which I took as a threat and stopped asking questions, at least those kinds of questions.

"Deputy, where's that bottle?" Emmett said, suddenly taking a hand in the conversation.

"Huh? Oh, in the bottom drawer," Joshua said before realizing what it was he'd just said. "Say, listen—"

But it was no use. In a wink Emmett had snatched up the bottle and taken a long swig from it, passing it on to his compadres, who each did the same. By the time he put it back in the drawer it was half empty.

"Now that I will charge you for," Pa said, still testy.

"And I'll gladly pay you for it," Emmett said with a smile. "Until that time, if you'll give us back our hardware we'll be the first to volunteer for your posse."

"You? Volunteer?" Chance said in surprise.

"Why sure," Emmett said, still smiling that devilish way he had. "You ain't got no competition around here for a decent fistfight. And we ain't been in a good shootout in some time now."

"Well, now," Chance said, a smile coming to his own face now, "there may be hope for you yet." The man had expressed my brother's own firm philosophy about fighting: If you can't find a good one around, do a little traveling until you come across a good foofaraw.

Too Many Drifters

Joshua dug into one of the desk drawers and pulled out the pistols Emmett and his friends had deposited the afternoon before when they'd checked in as guests for the night.

"Good," Emmett said once he had his six-gun back again. Patting it at his side, he added, "Don't feel so necked no more."

"Anybody else in this town who'll volunteer?" Bond asked as we headed for the door. The man got the answer to his question just outside the marshal's office.

Sitting astride their horses were the Wilson brothers, Tom and Jeremiah, and four other young men from Twin Rifles and the vicinity. Tom and Jeremiah Wilson, although a mite tamer than Chance or I had turned out to be, were still a reliable pair to depend on in a pinch. They'd proven that not long ago with their daddy up in Hogtown. But that's a whole 'nother canyon. No doubt about it, we had our posse.

"What're we waiting for?" Tom asked.

"Good question," I said, and without another word all but two of us headed for the livery stables to saddle and ride.

Chance and Emmett made their way to Kelly's Hardware and picked up a whole passel of ammunition.

CHAPTER
★ 14 ★

If the tracks we were following were right, they had headed for John Fitch's place. I'd been a Texas Ranger long enough before the war to know that there is no accounting for the things a man afoul of the law will do. Absolutely none. Chance, Pa, and me had seen instances where men would fight to the last to keep all of fifty dollars from a theft of some sort. Then there were others who would get a good case of guilt and walk right in and turn themselves over to the law when they could have gotten away scot-free. There was just no telling. I'd given it some thought once and come to the conclusion that these fellows who thought they were wily as a fox had outfoxed themselves. As for the reason Phineas McDougal had headed for the Fitch place, well, the only thing I could come up with was it was in the line of his retreat.

We topped the rise before the Fitch place and reined in our mounts.

"I figure half a dozen of 'em," Chance said.

"Seven," Emmett corrected him. "Six riders plus the fat man."

"Yeah, I noticed one pair of tracks run pretty deep," I said. The fat man was obviously Phineas McDougal. Or someone carrying a hell of a lot of gold coins.

"Think they circled the Fitch's?" Tom Wilson asked. "The tracks lead straight down the road to the farmhouse."

A rifle shot rang out from the farmhouse, kicking up dust in front of us. Our horses got real shy at that.

"No, that's them," I said, pulling my reins in tighter.

"How can you be sure?" Bond asked.

"Hoss, John Fitch wouldn't have missed." I looked at my brother and said, "Chance, I'm gonna take Emmett, Compton, and the Wilson brothers with me and circle around to the barn. There's got to be an advantage in getting closer. How about you take the rest and circle the other direction."

"You're reading my mind, brother," was all he said before he started giving directions like he was a cavalry sergeant again. Sometimes I wonder if situations like this don't bring out the past in all of us, especially that part of us that was hooked up with some war along the line.

By the time we had made our way to the back of the barn, we all had our rifles out and ready for action. The trouble was there had been a couple of shots fired in our direction as we rode, and they'd come from the barn.

"It looks like we'll have to do some housecleaning before we'll get inside that barn," I said as I dismounted, rifle in hand. "What do you think?" I said to anyone interested.

"Me and Jeremiah will work our way around the sides of the barn in case they try escaping that way," Tom Wilson said. "Flush 'em out and we'll pot shot 'em for you."

"Sounds good," Emmett said, the authority showing in his voice even though he lacked the stripes to go along with it.

I seriously doubted that the birds inside would try to make any kind of an escape out the front of the barn, not if they'd seen us sitting atop that rise. I suspicioned all of them had seen us before we'd come down. If they knew we were at their back door, they'd likely know that there were more of us at the front door of both the house and the barn.

Unlike the wide front doors of the barn, the back only had one regular-sized door, and it was that we would have to enter by. Emmett and I were each on opposite sides of the door, Compton behind me, when there was a noise from an open door above us that led to the hayloft.

Compton must have been trying to impress us, or else he was pure crazy. Quick as could be, he ran out in plain sight, brought his rifle up to his shoulder, and shot a man who was standing above us in the opening. His body tumbled forward, landing in a thud about six feet in front of the door. Compton had a smile on his face, for he'd done well in getting one of the culprits. But it was a mistake.

The back door to the barn burst open and out stepped one of the men I briefly recognized as one of the drifters Emmett and I had met up by Horse Trap Canyon the other day. He was about as friendly looking now as he had been back then, only this time he had a six-gun in his fist. He shot Compton once in the chest before I could bring my Colt revolving rifle down and pull the trigger. The end of my barrel wasn't but a foot from his own chest, and the shot sent him reeling backward inside the barn.

Emmett rushed inside, his pistol in one hand, rifle in the other, both guns blazing before he was a foot inside the door. I don't know how in the hell he saw anything in there, but I was in right behind him and there were two dead men on the floor by the time my eyes adjusted to the darkness.

John's children must have been held as hostages in the barn, for they both ran into my arms, crying.

"There now," I said, not knowing how I could comfort them. Hell, I had a rifle and six-gun in my fists and wasn't about to let go of them. But so far there were only three men down. "It's gonna be all right."

"They hit me," Marie said in a halting voice. I looked at her in what little light there was in the barn, glancing down at the two dead men, then back at the fourteen-year-old girl.

"Don't you worry, darling," I said in as soft a voice as I could muster, "they ain't never gonna do that again." I held them both tight for a minute before realizing that there was still a bunch of shooting going on toward the house. And that there was a man out back who had risked his life for these children and come out on the short end of it in the process. "Listen, I want you two to tell Sergeant Emmett here what they were up to," I said and nodded toward the big man. "He's on our side and he's here to help."

Then I went out back to see if I could help Compton. He turned out to be a real trooper after all. Still had hold of his rifle, he did. His free hand was covering the hole in his chest, blood seeping out through the cracks in his fingers, as though the man were trying desperately to plug up the hole in a dam.

"I got him, didn't I?" he asked, breathing slowly now.

"Damn sure betcha," I said, feeling a lump in my throat. I'd misjudged the man, misjudged him terribly. All I could think of was how I needed to make it all up to him. There wasn't any way. "You're a helluva trooper, Compton, you know that, don't you?" I said, knowing it was only a small measure of what the man was worth.

"Alex," he said, his voice getting softer, his breath slower. "Gotta get the tombstone right, huh?"

"Hey, Alex, I'm gonna buy you the biggest . . ." I started to say, but I never knew whether he heard me or not. By the time I got the words out he was dead. I set his head down gently, put his bloody hand around the rifle, which was now held almost at the port arms position. The man was still a soldier and deserved at least that kind of respect.

I felt a fire burning in me that I hadn't felt in a long time, felt it grow and grow. What fed it was the killing of Alex Compton, a good but misunderstood man. Somebody was going to die for this. Somebody in John Fitch's house! I had to save the Fitches the way we'd saved their children. I couldn't let them die the way Alex Compton had. They were friends and too close to let die a needless death.

"Here," I said, shoving my Colt rifle into Emmett's arms. "How many shots left in your pistol?" I wasn't asking, I was giving commands now.

"Three," the stunned man replied. "But I'll fix that right quick." He seemed to know what I had in mind and had his spare cylinder out and replaced in less than a minute's time.

"Can you cover me until I get to the house?"

"Hell, Wash, I been doing that for a living for damn near twenty years," was all he said. "Good luck with whatever it is, son."

They were still firing out the front window of John's house, but they pulled back their rifles real quick as soon as Emmett was firing in their direction. It gave me a good deal of confidence as I worked my way toward the front of the house. But then I wasn't worried about luck. That didn't have a damn thing to do with it. I was killing mad, and that was the only thing I had left to do that day, the only thing.

There was no one at the front window by the time I reached the porch, although it was hard telling where they were inside. I undid the thong in John's front door and gave it a push as three bullets came flying out the door in my direction. I backed up against the wall of the front of the house, noticing for the first time how hard I was breathing.

"Fill your hand!" I yelled and busted inside the

house, guns blazing. My first shot hit one of their chairs, which was empty. The second one went wild somewhere, I don't know. I was too busy trying to get a fix on what was taking place inside the house.

"No, please, don't!" I heard John scream, then saw the man he was speaking to as he pulled the trigger of his six-gun. I was moving inside the house now, shooting at the man, spinning him around with two shots, hoping the son of a bitch died before he hit the floor. John was on the floor, Greta kneeling over him.

"Wash!" I looked up and saw Chance rushing down the hall, apparently having come through the back door. I spotted one man flat up against the wall, waiting for my brother to rush in so he could kill him. I shot him twice before I felt the pain high in my back. I wanted to turn to find out who had done it to me, but Chance beat me to it. Once inside the house, he simply stopped dead in his tracks, held out two pistols at arm's length, and shot in my direction. The bullets whizzed past my head and I felt more than heard the sound of them hitting their object. The man was half falling on me as I turned to my side, catching him as he fell on my shoulder. If he wasn't dead, he should have been.

"What's the matter, couldn't save any of these pilgrims for me?" my brother asked, standing there with a grin on his face like the cat who's just eaten the bird. But then that's my brother.

Emmett burst through the door and in a flash had his rifle trained on the one last culprit in the living room. "You're dead, mister," he said as he took aim on him.

But Phineas McDougal was a coward after all.

"No! No! Don't shoot me!" he all but yelled.

Emmett glanced at me and must have seen the look on my face, knowing that I felt a lot worse.

"Fine by me, mister," he said, moving forward and bringing his rifle butt up into the fat man's stomach. When Phineas McDougal bent forward, Emmett slammed the rifle butt down against the man's back, watching him fall face first to the floor. "You'll just wish you was dead."

"Looks like the money's back here," I heard Bond say.

"You need some tending to, little brother," Chance said, a look of caution about him. To Greta he said, "How's John?"

"I'm afraid John is dead," I heard her say, crying the words she spoke.

CHAPTER
★ 15 ★

What do you mean, I need looking after?" I asked, confused.

"This," Chance said and, holstering one of his pistols, reached up over my left shoulder and brought away a hand smeared with blood.

"Jesus, Mary and Joseph," I murmured when I glanced at the area of my shoulder he'd just touched. There is something about the sight of your own blood that makes a body a mite more queasy than usual, and I was feeling that right now.

"Looks like he got you from behind, son," Emmett said, taking note of my shoulder wound before giving the floor a quick glance. When I looked down at what he'd seen, I saw a Bowie knife laying next to the man

Chance had killed, the man who had cut me from behind. Suddenly my arm was feeling a good deal of pain that hadn't been there before and I found myself bearing a stiffness that wasn't there prior to this fight. "Here, let me help you with that," Emmett added as he set down his shotgun and started to work his way around me.

But a knife wound wasn't uppermost in my mind and I was at Greta's side before Emmett could help me. John Fitch had died from the gunshot wound to his chest, a scene I doubted Greta would ever forget. Pa said he still had nightmares of the day he'd found Ma's body outside the ranch house Chance and I had rebuilt and now lived in. Somehow I knew he'd never forget that scene in his mind, just as I knew Greta would constantly live with the last thought of the lifeless man now cradled in her lap.

"I don't know what to say, Greta," I said. Pa claims I'm a lot more compassionate than my brother and maybe he's right, but at the moment I couldn't think of anything else to say, no more than either Pa or Chance likely would. Seeing a loved one die isn't the easiest of situations to deal with in life.

Whatever she was going to say never sounded, for as soon as the children appeared in the doorway they seemed to sense there was something wrong. Their eyes focused on their mother and father and they were at their side in no time.

"Papa!" Marie cried and all but buried herself in her father's chest. The fact that there was blood all over the place didn't seem to phase her at all now.

"Daddy!" was Stephen's exclamation, and he was soon doing the same as his sister. Despite the pain I was feeling in my shoulder, I wanted to hug them all, show them that I was feeling just as much pain at John's loss as they were.

"McHale, check that kitchen area for some hot water," Emmett said, the sergeant in him taking charge now. "And ary there ain't—"

"I know, boil some," McHale replied and set about his task.

"Come on, boy, you set yourself down on this stoop and let me get that shirt off'n you. Bleed to death ary you don't." Emmett was clearly putting himself in charge, although he needn't have. Even feeling as faint as I was, I could see the men who'd come along on our posse going about the house, each doing his own bit to make things right, make things easier for Greta and her children—setting furniture back in place, pulling bloodied bodies out of the house to give the vultures a chance at them—all while Emmett looked after me.

"You say you found the money?" I asked my brother.

"That's what I heard," was Chance's reply. "Ought to make the town real happy. Make a hero out of you too."

Chance was grinning at this last statement, but I wasn't feeling funny about anything at the moment. In a serious tone, I said, "Chance, you and me been in enough scrapes in that damned war to know heroes ain't nothing more than storybook material."

"Yeah," my brother said in a somber tone, the grin now gone, "I reckon you're right."

It went on like that for about an hour, the house a hive of activity as it was fixed up as best as possible into the condition it had been in before our confrontation with McDougal and his men. Me, I sat at the kitchen table and drank some coffee Emmett had served up.

Greta and her children had been taken back to her bedroom, the lot of them laying down on John and Greta's bed. An hour later, when I'd first set down at the table to have some coffee, Greta came into the kitchen.

"Your men are too kind, Wash," she said, apparently having regained a good deal of her composure. She was a strong one, this woman.

Before I could respond, Emmett had stepped in, once again proving he was the man in charge. "Nonsense, ma'am, we'd do it for anyone." Then, taking the woman by the shoulders, looking her square in the eyes, he said in a stern tone, "You get back in there and lay down, ma'am. You're gonna need your rest. Besides, ary no one told you, I'm the best damn cook the cavalry ever had."

"No, Sergeant," she said, apparently picking up on how one of the men had addressed Emmett, "I must do something. There is always too much to do. Too much."

"Well, in that case, ma'am, I got a notion this would be a good time for some stew," Emmett suggested.

"You are too kind, Sergeant. But yes, stew would feed a good deal of men. Your men."

Greta went about gathering up the necessary ingredients while Emmett found and sharpened a knife for his use. After a while the smell of stew filled the air and Emmett and Greta were the only ones really doing any work. A second pot of coffee had been made, and the rest of us were taking it in now as the stew simmered. It was only midafternoon but we hadn't had a noon meal, so the stew would be a welcome feast.

While everyone else had been busy with one thing or another, I'd been thinking. I waited until Chance, Emmett, and the others took a break before speaking my mind.

"Remember those yahoos we met down by Horse Trap Canyon the other day, Emmett?" I asked.

"Yeah. A couple of 'em were out in the barn, as I recall. What about it?"

"Well, that's just it—there was only a *couple,*" I said.

Emmett as well as the others seemed puzzled by my words.

"Just how far you taking me down the trail before you show me the fork in the road, son?" Emmett asked with a frown.

"I don't know about you, hoss, but I got the distinct feeling that those birds fought in groups."

"True," Emmett said, stroking his jaw in thought but still sporting a confused look about him.

"This is my brother's roundabout way of asking where the others are now if they ain't here," Chance said, catching on to my train of thought. He gave me a look and shook his head, a sly grin beginning to appear on his face as he said, "He's the only man I ever knew who'd reach around his ass to scratch his elbow."

"Yeah, I see what you mean," Emmett said, and the others nodded ascent as well. "Those birds were kind of close. But I swear none of 'em looked like he was brother to the others. Yeah, you're right about that, Wash."

"What's on your mind, Wash?" Tom Wilson asked.

"Well, if we got rid of three of 'em, where in the hell are the other four? If there's only four. There could be more."

"I'll bite. Where?" my brother asked, his curiosity up.

"Remember when Pa made us deputies and all that hogwash he gave us about his badge only being good within the city limits?" I said.

"Sure. Still sounds strange," Chance replied. "I never thought Pa would turn down a chance to fight a fight. It just ain't like him."

"But what if he *didn't* turn down a chance to get into a good fight?" I asked in pure speculation.

"Maybe I've been riding too many wild mustangs, son, but you're gonna have to explain what it is you're spouting off about," Emmett said, scratching his head. "You're flat out losing me."

"I think Pa was ahead of us all the time," I said, setting down my coffee cup. "I think Pa stayed in town because he knew Phineas McDougal was a greedy man and would want whatever money was left in town as well as what he'd stolen from his own bank."

"Yeah," Emmett said, suddenly catching on to the whole thing. "More'n likely them other four are back in your town trying to hold up the other bank. Yeah, now I see what you're driving at."

"Boots and saddles!" Chance said, immediately pushing his chair back from the table and rising to his full height. The old cavalryman was back in him now and he was ready to ride, the afternoon's action apparently not being enough for him. Emmett was right there beside him too.

"Just hold your horses, boys!" I all but yelled as the rest of them got to their feet. "It's a waste of time."

"What're you talking about, boy?" Emmett said excitedly.

"Yeah, they could be robbing our bank right now!" Chance threw in, just as anxious to get going.

I pulled out my pocket watch and checked it. "First off, it's past three o'clock and the bank is closed," I said. "If they ain't robbed it by now, they won't do it until tomorrow morning when it's about to open. Second, if they've already robbed the bank there ain't a helluva lot we can do about it at the moment. Those mounts of ours ain't worth spit right now any more than we are. They're needing rest just like us. Besides," I added in a tone of finality, "if they tried taking that bank, you can bet the people in Twin Rifles ain't gonna wait for us to get back to let someone else get away with their money. Not twice!"

Everything I said was true and they knew it. But it was Greta who settled the whole argument.

"Gentlemen, if you do not sit, I do not serve," were the only words she spoke, and powerful words they were indeed. You never saw as many men grab hold of seating space as the lot of us did then.

There was something to what Emmett had said about being a good cook, for the stew was a good meal about which none of us complained. No man with his mouth full of food this good ever had a chance to complain. During the meal I felt a new surge of energy within me, almost as though the stew, biscuits, and coffee were enough alone to renew my strength. I found myself feeling glad about it too, for I was going to need it for what I had in mind.

Greta woke the children just before we left, which was about an hour before sunset that night. Each of them came to Emmett and me and gave us a hug, thanking us for what we'd done for them.

"Oh my God!" Marie said, a look of surprise about her.

"What is it, darlin'?" Emmett asked with a look of concern appearing on his own face.

"Nightmare!" she almost screamed before a hand came to her mouth.

"Nightmare?" Emmett seemed to spend most of that afternoon in a confused mood.

"She's talking about a mustang we broke for her the other day," Chance said.

"Yes, is he all right? Did he get—"

"That big old piece of work out in the corral?" Emmett said. "Why, there ain't nothing wrong with him atall. Fit as a fiddle, as Grandma used to put it." Emmett then grabbed the girl and brought her to him, holding her as though she were his own. "He's just fine, sweetheart, just fine," he added in a lower voice.

Greta was sending her children off to bed about the time we mounted up to head for town. I assured her that I'd have the undertaker come out the next day and talk to her about funeral arrangements and that Chance and I would check on her periodically.

I reckon we had one of the most beautiful sunsets I'd ever seen that evening. The thing of it is, I don't recall much about it.

I reckon it's because I had other things on my mind.

CHAPTER
★ 16 ★

It was dark by the time we reached the edge of town. We didn't ride in like we usually did. Not this time. If my suspicions about Pa were correct, Twin Rifles wasn't anything like the town I'd left earlier in the day—not in the way of population, anyway, if you get my drift. We dismounted at the edge of town, taking nothing but our weapons with us as we entered Twin Rifles, and that we did like a cougar on the hunt: quiet and light-footed.

"How do you want to do this?" Tom Wilson asked.

"Seems to me we ought to check in with Pa first," I said, not waiting for Chance to speak up, knowing full well that he'd want to charge in like some bull having a red flag waved at him. Me, I'd seen enough carnage to last me more than a lifetime in my days with the Confederacy, and the killing that had taken place today wasn't making me feel better about anymore to come. "If anyone knows what's going on in this town, he will."

"He's right," Chance said to the group in agreement, a rarity for the man when dealing with me. "I've got a notion we're dealing with more than just those yahoos Emmett and Wash say they met up with. A lot more."

"Yeah, and don't forget this buzzard," Emmett threw in, yanking a tied and gagged Phineas McDougal alongside him. When we'd left the Fitch place it was agreed that McDougal should be the sole responsibility of Emmett until we could get him to a cell in jail. McDougal was within hearing range of the agreement when it was made and it scared the bejesus out of him, so much so that he hadn't uttered a peep on our way into Twin Rifles, not even when we'd asked him some rather pointed questions about what it was he was trying to do to this town. "We got to find a place to bed him down for the night." Even though they were said in a low tone, Emmett growled the words rather than spoke them, ramming an elbow into the fat man's side when he'd gotten them out. No one paid any attention to Phineas McDougal's grunt, for the man knew what we thought of him by now, which wasn't a hell of a lot.

We made our way down a back alley, then carefully past the rear of several town establishments to the jail, making certain there weren't any guards to alert any others to our presence. I couldn't tell you what it was that made me hesitate outside the back door to Pa's jail, but I did. Maybe it was the feeling of overcautiousness I was suddenly aware of within me. The comment my brother had made about a force of men larger than we were anticipating didn't set well with me at all, basically because a lot of the time Chance and his gut feelings were right on the money. Whatever it was, I was glad.

I had my six-gun in hand when I slowly opened the door, hoping either Pa or Joshua had oiled the squeak in it. Apparently they had, for the door opened without so much as a sound and I entered quietly, unaware of who was behind me. I couldn't tell who the man I spotted was or what his business was, although I had a good suspicion. All I knew then was that the man standing close to the holding cells had a gun trained on Pa and Joshua, and that wasn't any too friendly an act. But he had his back to me and that was all that mattered at the moment.

I was contemplating whether to stick a gun in his ribs or crack his skull as I inched closer to him when old Charlie, the town drunk, made up my mind for me. Charlie must have had an early evening, for he was lying there in the cell Pa always left vacant for him. It was when he rolled over and mumbled something to himself that he caught the gunman's attention. As the man turned to see what it was Charlie was up to, I tossed my six-gun over to my left hand and let fly a hard right at the gunman, catching him totally off guard and knocking him askew as he tumbled over a chair to his rear. He'd made the mistake of thinking he could take care of Pa and Joshua without tying them up, so they were at his side by the time he was sprawled out on the floor. I got the impression they were a mite mad at the man too, for as soon as Pa had scooped up the gunman's pistol Joshua had grabbed him with his own fists and was beating the tar out of him. When I caught a glance of the bruise on Joshua's cheek, I didn't blame him one bit.

"Whassa commotion all 'bout?" Charlie slurred from his cell.

"Nothing, Charlie," Pa said with a mad growl, "we're just putting away another ruffian. Go back to sleep, Charlie."

"Thanksh, Will. You're a good man."

"So are you, Charlie, so are you," I said with a smile. I'd wait until later, when the man was sober, to explain just what I meant by that comment.

"Where in thunder have you boys been?" Pa asked with the same gruffness with which he'd spoken to the town drunk. Chance and me gave one another disbelieving looks. It was the second time that day Pa had taken to confusing us with his words. By the tone of his voice, you'd think we'd been out for nothing more than an afternoon stroll.

"Why, shooting up the people that stole your money, of course," Emmett said, cocking a daring eye at my father. "What'd you think we were doing, Marshal?"

The Wilson brothers tossed the money we'd recovered onto the floor in front of Pa. "Got it all back too," Tom said with a wink and a nod that reminded me of Asa Wilson, Tom and Jeremiah's father. It was fall of last year that we'd made our way up to a place called Hogtown to get Tom and his brother out of a fix. Asa had gotten killed in the process, but seeing Tom take on one of his father's characteristics, I thought the old man would be mighty proud of his boys for what they'd helped accomplish today. Mighty proud.

"The posse made it back all right," I said. Then, on a sadder note, I added, "But John Fitch is dead."

"What?" Pa was more surprised than anything, I thought. On the other hand, he'd been a friend of John Fitch's as long—or longer—than Chance or me, so it likely hurt more to hear of the man's death.

I took the time to explain to Pa what had happened on our ride after the bank robbers while Emmett bodily threw Phineas McDougal into a vacant cell. The now battered gunman went into a separate cell.

"That's a shame," Pa said in a soft voice when I was through talking. "He was a good man. Had a lot of dreams for this land."

I'd been feeling too much pain that afternoon to dwell on John Fitch's death. Then there was the ride back to town, and my mind was filled with thoughts of what we would do once we got to Twin Rifles. Pa's words had sounded like a eulogy of sorts. Perhaps they were. Suddenly the thought of death was upon me again, but not John's death. My gaze turned to Phineas McDougal in his cell, and a whole wall of hate filled me up inside. I could barely feel the pain in my shoulder now, I was that filled with hatred for this man.

"You know, mister, you brought an awful lot of grief and dying to the people of this town," I said as I grabbed the keys off the hook and opened the fat man's cell. I tossed the keys to Joshua and walked in the cell, the urge to kill coming over me. "You come here to steal our money. You brought men with you who seem to hire out to kill and do your dirty work for you. But when they kill a man, you ain't even got the guts to stand up and take the responsibility for it. Well, Phineas, I want some answers to where the rest of your gang is, and I want 'em now. You and your kind ain't gonna kill nobody in this town anymore."

"And if I don't give you the answers you want?" he said, trying to put on a front that anyone could see was false bravado.

I slammed my right fist into my left hand. The shock going up my left arm made me suddenly painfully aware that I'd been wounded that afternoon. Still, it didn't seem to matter. Not now.

"Then you'll die knowing you were loyal to your bunch," I said through gritted teeth. "Of course, they more than likely won't know and will care less, but I wouldn't worry about that, Phineas, because you're gonna talk." I ran a fist into my hand again for effect. "Now, where are they?"

Nobody else was trying to stop me, for all I could hear was my own voice filling the room. McDougal made what came out like an annoying sound, which was just how I took it. Since I wasn't in the mood to take any guff from the man, I hit him hard across the face, knocking him back against the cell bars.

"What did you do that—" he started to say, and I hit him again, this time in the stomach, which he sure had enough of. I felt my fist go several inches into his soft gut, hitting him hard enough so as to pin him against the bars again. My left hand wasn't worth all that much in a fight now, but I had enough strength in it to grab him by the throat and hold him against the bars while I pounded my right fist into the man's ribs and again across the face.

"Talk, you sorry sonofabitch!" I said with a gasp, not realizing how out of breath I was.

Phineas McDougal was now a desperate man. He was looking for help from Pa as he gazed over my shoulder. "You can't let him—" he started again, his words spitting blood on my own face as they dribbled from his mouth.

"I don't see nothing," Pa said, although it was clear he was looking straight at the two of us.

"Me neither," Joshua said with a straight face.

"Appears to me you and your boys are tangling with the wrong men, mister," Emmett said, a look of satisfaction about him.

Chance just stood there and smiled, likely thinking how badly he'd beat this man up if he were in my place. But like I said before, that's my brother.

I still had my hand around McDougal's throat. "I think I'll bust your nose next," I said and drew back my fist.

"No! Wait! Don't hit me!" Blood spattered over my face once more. The man was on the verge of crying from the looks of him.

"Then start talking," I growled, "and stop spitting that goddamn blood all over me."

It didn't take much effort to move him from the bars to his cot and plunk his sorry ass down on it. Pa tossed him a towel that was already dirty, but McDougal didn't seem to care, using it to wipe his bloodied face.

Then he talked.

Too Many Drifters

It seemed that his original plan had been to get as far away as possible with the money he'd absconded from the bank he'd opened, the idea being to draw the posse he knew would follow in his direction. While this was taking place some of the men who had drifted into Twin Rifles would get a look at the town and the Twin Rifles Bank and Trust. Then tomorrow, at 9:00 A.M. sharp, they would rob the bank as it opened.

"You know, Marshal, they should take your badge away for letting him beat me the way he just did," McDougal said to Pa once he was through talking. I reckon he was referring to the less than hospitable manner in which I'd treated him not long ago.

"Normally, mister, I'd have to agree with you," Pa said with a frown. "But when these men tell me you're responsible for the death of one of our people and you've had the audacity to steal our money to boot, well, I reckon there's exceptions to every rule."

"Don't seem to me you've considered the alternative, mister," Emmett said with an evil look about him.

"Alternative?" Phineas McDougal seemed awful confused, but then he'd been that way most of the day.

"Yeah. You see, in the outfit I come from we didn't take too many prisoners, so if I was the one dealing with you, well . . . you know how it is," Emmett said.

"You'd have killed me?" McDougal asked, a terrified look now gripping his face.

Emmett gave the man a devilish smile. "Old habits die hard." The words made the fat man seemingly shrink in size as he huddled back in the corner of his cell on his bunk. He wouldn't utter another word all night.

"Joshua, I think it's about time we had us another pot of coffee boiling," Pa said, now taking charge of the situation.

"I was thinking the very same thing, Will," the deputy said in agreement.

Pa and Chance and me had all been pretty good Texas Rangers before the war had split us up and we'd each gone our separate ways. But there was something about having a badge on my chest that made it seem as though we were all working together again, just like we had in those old days, those days with the Texas Rangers. Mind you, I knew those days were probably gone forever, but at that moment I felt a good deal of camaraderie in that office. I reckon that's why no one objected any when I added, "Yeah, we've got some bank robbers to catch."

CHAPTER
★ 17 ★

I knocked on the door. No answer. I knocked again, hoping I was only going to rouse the occupant and not the entire neighborhood. Chance and I had worked our way to the north side of town, where most of the residences were located. The south side of town had a couple of small wooded areas and some creek water outside of it, but for the most part the north side was where the people who had decided to reside in our fair town had built their homes. I knocked again. This time I waited a while as someone inside the house began to stir. Then a light went on and soon found its way to the front door.

"Who is it? What do you want?" Even half asleep Walter Lawrence's voice sounded all business. But then I imagine that was the nature of the man, being a banker and all.

"It's Wash and Chance Carston," I said in a whisper. "Open up, we've got to see you." The light moved over to the front window and a curtain was cautiously pulled back as Walter Lawrence gave us each a disgruntled glare. Then the curtain fell back into its original position and I heard the sound of a door being unbolted and slowly opened.

"Good Lord, man," Walter Lawrence said, his disposition still all business, "do you know what time it is? Why, it must be—"

"Around midnight, I reckon," Chance said.

"Yes, midnight at least." It didn't take much to know that the banker wasn't used to being roused at this time of the night. A good sound sleep was likely what this man was used to. "Now what is it you two want?"

"Need to talk to you about your bank, Mr. Lawrence," Chance said in as tactful a manner as he was ever likely to muster.

"My bank!" the man all but exploded. He then took great care in gritting his teeth in the manner you might see those stage actors do when they portray the evil banker foreclosing the mortgage on the fair maiden. I was tempted to mention to him that he'd been seeing too many of those melodrama shows but thought better of it for the moment. "Don't you know that's what I have banking hours for? Tell me, are you two simply stupid or drunk? Or both?"

The look on my brother's face said he'd given up all hope of being tactful with the man. Even in the half moon I could see his brows knit together as a frown came to his face now. "I thought Pa said this man was easy to get along with."

I shrugged. "That's what he said. Maybe you should tell him that we're here about someone robbing his bank."

Suddenly Walter Lawrence reminded me an awful lot of Old Ass Buster, the wild mustang we'd had some trouble with the other day. Not that I'd call the man a horse face, you understand, but I've got to tell you he let out about as much air as that mustang did when Emmett kicked him in the stomach. I had the notion that mentioning the possibility of losing money from his bank was the equivalent of kicking Walter Lawrence in the gut.

"Phineas McDougal just broke down and told us when the rest of his gang is going to be trying to rob the Twin Rifles Bank and Trust," I said. "At nine o'clock tomorrow morning."

"Please come in, won't you?" he said, suddenly grateful for us spreading the word. In no time we were in his house and seated at a table, explaining to the banker what it was we had in mind. Chance and I were quick about explaining the trap we were planning to set in order to catch these yahoos in the morning. Once we were through, we bid our good-byes and left as quietly as we'd entered. Walter Lawrence promised he'd be there half an hour earlier than usual, ready to cooperate with us on this mission.

We were both yawning by the time we got back to the jail, ready to fall asleep wherever we could find the room to lay down.

"Mr. Lawrence knows what's gonna take place tomorrow morning, Pa," I said, pouring my last cup of coffee for the night. "How about the rest of you guys?"

Pa had kept the rest of the posse members in the jail as my brother and I had finished our mission to Walter Lawrence's house, discussing with them how he fashioned handling this situation tomorrow morning. I was sure that in the back of each of our minds was the doubt about just how many men we would encounter at 9:00 A.M. tomorrow morning. I knew that the thought was heavy on my own mind.

Chance seemed to handle it by breaking down his six-guns on Pa's desk and cleaning them as best he could, checking to make sure all the loads were in place once he was done. I followed suit with my own revolver but couldn't seem to get the events of the next day out of my mind. Would I be shot up worse tomorrow than I was today? Would I see the sunset tomorrow night? Would I be alive tomorrow night? All of these were questions I couldn't answer.

"Why don't you get some sleep, son?" I heard Pa say as he put a firm hand on my shoulder later that night. "You're gonna need all the sleep you can muster, especially with that wound of yours." I hadn't heard this tone of voice from Pa in many a year and suddenly had a great appreciation for the man and his being.

"Yeah, I reckon you're right." If I sounded a bit depressed about the whole thing, it was because I was.

"It's gonna be all right, son," Pa added. "We'll make it through this fracas just like we always do. You'll see."

Chance holstered his Colt Army Model .44 and pushed his hat back on his head.

"Come on, brother, there's a couple of empty cots back there we can get a mite of shuteye on."

I didn't think I'd be able to sleep that night, but as soon as my head hit the pillow I was out.

CHAPTER
★ 18 ★

The streets were deserted as could be early that morning as the sun came up on Twin Rifles. Usually, about the only time you'd see our main street this uninhabited was on Sunday mornings when everyone was at church. But today wasn't Sunday by a long shot, and as the town came to life there only seemed to be a minimum of citizens on the streets or traveling down the boardwalk here and there. If you thought about it real careful like, you'd swear that something unexpected was in the air, and you'd be right.

We'd gotten up way before first light, Pa making sure we each had a cup of coffee to bring us fully awake. Then, one by one, we'd made our way over to

Big John Porter's cafe in the darkness and were fed an early breakfast. From there it was a matter of positioning ourselves for the attempted robbery we knew was coming. Pa, Chance, and me had taken up stations inside the bank so as to get the drop on the men McDougal had told us would be showing up to rob the Twin Rifles Bank and Trust. Emmett and his boys would work their way up the alleys on either side of the bank once the outlaws had entered town, ready to throw down on these culprits as soon as the ball commenced.

"When are they going to be here?" Walter Lawrence said, nervously snapping shut his pocket watch and placing it back in his pocket for what seemed like the hundredth time. "It's a quarter to nine. When are they going to be here?"

"Don't you worry, Walter," Pa said to the bank manager in a soothing voice. "I got a notion they'll be here right on the dot. You mark my words."

"He's right, Mr. Lawrence," I said. "Greedy men are like that." I shouldn't have had to say it (bankers being some of the greediest men on this earth), but Walter Lawrence was a jumble of nerves. The tall man had been this way ever since he'd arrived at the bank to open up. His faith and confidence were overwhelming, to say the least. Or maybe I should have known that I was dealing with a banking man, and people like Walter Lawrence make a living out of being nervous over their money.

"I just wish it was all over with," he added. If he knew how to roll a cigarette, I do believe he would have.

"Here they come," I said a few minutes later as I looked out from behind the curtain to the front window. I'd taken a gander in each direction, noticing that they had come in two groups, each group numbering five men, one from the north and one from the south side of town. They seemed to meet and converge right in front of the bank.

"All right, Walter," Pa said to the banker, "get out of sight and stay there." It wasn't a request, it was an order. The man did as he was told and crouched behind the desk he was usually found at. Pa, Chance, and me did some crouching of our own, right behind the three teller cages.

When they tried the door, they found it unlocked, just as we'd planned. I could only hear the door open, then the spurs of a handful of men jingling across the floor as they entered.

It was then we made our move, each of us popping up behind the teller cage. I thought I saw five of them, each with a gun in his hand. What they saw was Pa, Chance, and me, each of us with two six-guns pointed at them.

"No withdrawals today, boys," Pa said, quick and to the point. He never was one to mince words when it came to getting things done.

"Drop the guns or you're in real trouble," Chance said as he cocked both his Colt Army Model .44s.

If I could have thought of anything smart to say at the time I would have. But I didn't. By the time Pa and my brother got through spouting off, these fellows had made up their mind as to what they were going to do.

"It's a trap!" one of them yelled out as loud as he

could before attempting to fire his six-gun. His words were loud enough to warn the others outside, but attempting to fire his gun was as far as he got. I shot him twice, blood flowing from his chest like two tiny rivers as he slumped to the floor and died.

Two more of his crowd did the same, trying their damnedest to shoot us, but they only met with similar deaths. Like me, Chance had fired both of his guns at the same time, killing one of them. Pa, on the other hand, had always claimed that if you couldn't do it with one shot you didn't deserve anymore. One was all he needed to do in his man.

The remaining two lost their bravery real quick and turned tail to run. Both turned a hard right as they ran out the door, toward their mounts I was sure, when I heard the sound of two shots outside the bank. The two would-be bandidos staggered backward a step or two and fell to the boardwalk in silence. From the side of the alley I saw Emmett appear in front of one of the windows, sporting two of the Colt Army Model revolvers just like my brother's. Gunsmoke curled up from the ends of the barrels now, evidence that it was he who had done the shooting.

A massive amount of gunfire erupted across the street as I ran out the front door of the bank, taking long strides over the dead men inside to get there. I didn't have to look about to know that the rifle and pistol fire was coming from a number of rooftops in town, as well as alleyways. The Wilson brothers and a handful of other volunteers we'd rounded up during the night were the ones doing the firing, and what they were shooting at were the other half of the so-called gang that had ridden into town. But by the looks of them, the remaining five had been quick to heed their partners' advice and lit a shuck like a fox being discovered in the chicken coop. Not sticking around to help their compadres out of the jam they'd gotten into, all they'd left behind was a cloud of dust as they'd skedaddled out of town.

"Come on, boys, on your feet," Emmett was saying to the two men he'd shot. To me, he added, "Lordy, you'd think they'd been shot or something." They had indeed been shot but not as seriously as their friends inside the bank. One had taken a bullet in the leg, while the other had taken a slug high in his right arm. "The jail's right across the street over there."

The two men were stumbling across the street toward the hoosegow when I thought I heard a pair of horses riding away from the area, and it sounded like they'd come from behind the jail. I found myself picking up the pace, taking longer strides as Pa and Chance soon caught up with me. A distraught Joshua met us at the entrance to the jail.

"I tell you, Will, it was terrible, just terrible," the deputy said in a low, humbling voice.

"What are you talking about, Joshua?" Pa asked as we entered his office.

As soon as we entered the building, it was apparent that no more questions need be asked. Phineas McDougal and the man who'd taken a good beating from Joshua the night before were gone. Theirs must have been the horses I'd heard racing away behind the jail just now.

"How'd it happen?" I asked.

Too Many Drifters

"Well, I was tidying up a mite, you know, cleaning up that mess we'd made last night, and I bent over to pick up that rag you'd throwed that fat man, remember, Will?"

Pa nodded silently.

"I reckon he'd tossed it in front of that other feller's cell, 'cause when I stooped down, why, he whisked the gun right outta my holster, he did." The only enthusiasm in Joshua's voice was that which wanted to get the whole sad episode over with as far as the telling went. It was obvious that the man had forced Joshua to unlock their cells and let them go. But the deputy wasn't in any mood to repeat what we all knew. Instead, he unpinned his badge and handed it to Pa. "I reckon you'll be wanting this," was all he said in that same humiliated voice.

"Oh, horse apples, Joshua," Pa said. "Ary I want your badge, why, you oughtta know by now that I'll be the one taking it off of you, and when I do you'll know. Right now I'm needing deputies something fierce."

"But Will, the place is empty!" Joshua said in surprise.

"Not anymore," Emmett said, pushing the two new prisoners in front of him as he entered the jail. "You got a couple of new occupants, if they don't bleed to death all over the place between here and there."

"Well now, I reckon I'll have to see about getting the doctor over here," Joshua said, suddenly acting as though the whole dreaded incident of which he'd been a part hadn't occurred.

"You do that," Pa said with a smile as his deputy grabbed his hat and left.

Tom Wilson stuck his head in next.

"I've got your horses out here if you want to do some riding," he said.

"Sure," Chance said, not waiting for me to answer. Then, giving me a glance, he added, "What do you say, brother?"

My shoulder was hurting again, but it didn't stop me from saying, "Let's ride."

CHAPTER
★ 19 ★

What's the fuss?" Charlie asked from his cell, sitting upright, stretching and rubbing his eyes as though nine-thirty were his normal rising time. But then maybe it was. I was just getting ready to leave when he spoke up.

"I swear you'd sleep through a twister ary one came through town, Charlie," Pa said with a frown. "Ain't you heard the shooting?"

"Is that what that was?" Charlie said, opening his eyes wide before squinting a second time. The light of day apparently had a hard time focusing in his eyes this early. "I thought I was dreaming about the Fourth of July."

"Hell no, you old scudder," Pa said with that backwoods growl he could work up. "Now see, ary you'd stop your drinking you'd get all sorts of informed about what goes on in this town."

"And what is that, my good man?" Charlie stretched again, opened his cell door, and wandered out to Pa's desk, opening the lower left drawer and pulling out Pa's bottle of whiskey. He took a good long swallow, sighed with relief, belched, and said, "Hair of the dog, you know." The whiskey bottle then went back in its place in the drawer.

"Why, the bank's been robbed and Will's boys done took off after 'em and got the money back," Joshua said in what I was sure was a tone meant to berate the town drunk. "John Fitch got himself killed once those yahoos got out to his place, but Chance and Wash got the money back, by God!"

I didn't know whether it was the swallow of whiskey that brought Charlie's sober side around or the news Joshua had been spouting off, but suddenly the man seemed as sober as a judge and paying just as much attention. "Did you say John Fitch is dead?" he asked in an astonished tone.

"Why, yes."

"Maybe you'd better tell me just what's taken place since the last time I hit the bottle," Charlie said. He was anything but playful or happy, the way a drunk tends to be, so Pa set about giving the man an abbreviated version of our discovery of Phineas McDougal's embezzlement activities, clear on up to this morning and the unsuccessful bank robbery.

"Wash, we've got to get a move on it," Tom Wilson said through the door. He was impatiently sitting on his horse out front. Me, I was standing almost in the doorway, half listening to Tom, half listening to what was taking place inside. "They're getting away, you know."

"I saw them horses they were riding when they came in to town, Tom," I said out the door. "They were pretty lathered up—close to being played out, if you ask me. Don't worry, they ain't going far."

As Pa was explaining the events of the last day or two, it crossed my mind that I didn't really know that much about Charlie. Hell, I didn't even know his last name! In a way he was like Joshua, a new addition to Twin Rifles by the time I'd returned from the war. Neither man had been here before Chance and I had left to fight the war, but like a handful of others, they had been here when we'd returned in May of '65. All I knew for sure about Charlie was that he was easy to get along with, especially if you bought him a drink. He also had a fair amount of tales to tell and, just like most drunks I'd come across, you couldn't tell where truth left off and imagination carried on. Of course, there are also a fair share of sober men who stretch the truth just as much. But the news of the death of John Fitch had hit this man pretty hard, and I found myself wondering why.

"I see," Charlie said once Pa was through talking. He scratched what must have been a three-day-old beard before saying, "I don't suppose you fellas would have a reasonably sober man with you on that posse?"

"Now what would you want to come along for?" I asked, just as curious as the rest in the room appeared to be.

Charlie blushed. "Well, old John, he bought me more than one beer, you know. Even a bottle once in a while. I reckon it just seems like I owe him something for that."

"Know what you mean, friend," said Emmett, who'd just stepped in the doorway next to me. "Can't say as I knew the man all that well, but he was indeed generous with his drinking money. Yes sir, losing someone who'll provide you with free booze, why that's a real loss."

"I don't know, Charlie," I said, shaking my head. "Are you sure you're steady enough to hold the reins of a horse, much less do any shooting if it comes to it? And I don't mind telling you I expect it'll come to it with these gunmen."

A look of disdain came over Charlie now, as though he weren't too keen about my doubting his abilities, and he quickly looked about the room. "Where is it now?" he mumbled to himself, then spotted an empty whiskey bottle in the trash bucket, picked it up, and began heading toward the front door. "No," he said to himself, then did an about face and marched toward the back door. "Come with me," he said on the way out, "and bring that cannon of yours with you, Wash."

"I wonder what he's up to," Joshua said.

Pa just shrugged his shoulders as he followed his deputy out the back door. Emmett's curiosity was up too, and he followed me.

"Don't want to scare the horses out front," Charlie said when we were out back. When none of us said anything, Charlie said to me, "I'm gonna trade you this bottle for your six-gun, Wash. Here."

I frowned in confusion as I took out my LeMat and handed it to the man, receiving his empty whiskey bottle in return.

"Toss that bottle somewhere in the air," he commanded, the six-gun in his fist at his side.

"Say when."

Charlie shrugged. "Any old time."

I waited a few seconds, then tossed it high in the air, about twenty-five feet out. The bottle reached its highest point when the sound of my LeMat went off and the empty whiskey bottle was no more, shattering into what seemed a million pieces before falling to the ground. When I looked down, there was Charlie, arm outstretched and holding my six-gun in his hand, steady as a rock. I didn't say a thing about the low whistles Pa and Joshua let out.

"There goes one more old soldier," Emmett said with what I thought to be an appreciative smile.

"In more ways than one," I said in a rather humble voice. I'd been in the army long enough to know that old-timers often called finishing off a bottle of whiskey "killing one more old soldier." If no one else understood, at least Emmett would. "I reckon you'll do, Charlie," I said, giving the man a slap on the back. "Think we can hunt up a pistol for him, Pa?"

"You bet."

It was somewhere around ten o'clock when we left that morning, but like I said, I wasn't worried. These birds had an hour's head start on us, but we had fresh horses and the ones they'd ridden into town looked like they'd been ridden awful hard just getting to Twin Rifles. If they were foolish enough to ride their mounts until they dropped, all they would accomplish would be walking across what could be some rather nasty ground.

Our posse, when we left town, consisted of Emmett,

Bond, McHale, the Wilson brothers, Chance, Charlie, and me. Pa wanted the others who'd been in our posse to stick close to town just in case these hombres doubled back and tried to rob the bank a second time once we were gone. It made sense so I didn't question it. You don't often question a man who is thirty-some years your senior, especially when he's your father.

We followed them out of town, soon picking up the fresh tracks of Phineas McDougal and his riding pard, the escapees from Pa's jail. The two had joined the five would-be bank robbers and were now all headed in the same direction.

I had a dark feeling about this whole thing, as though more killing was unavoidable and perhaps the wrong people would wind up getting killed. John Fitch had already died, although you wouldn't find me shedding a tear over any of the other killers we'd put to rest in the past two days. As my brother so callously put it once, the tears would dry rolling down my cheeks. It was when I saw Nightmare on the horizon that the dark feeling I had got worse. The horse was still saddled and that bothered me right off.

He seemed to know who we were, for he just stood there and waited for us to approach him. The whole thing gave me an eerie feeling and I felt the hair on my neck suddenly standing on end.

"Easy there, boy, easy now," Chance said, dismounting and walking up to the horse. Of all of us, he knew this mount best. I remembered back to the day he'd finished breaking him and the night we'd ridden over to the Fitch place for supper. Chance had made a present of Nightmare to Marie and Stephen.

Too Many Drifters

"What's the matter, Wash?" Emmett said, looking at me with a growing frown. "Something bothering you?"

"It's the girl and boy this steed belongs to," I said. "They're John Fitch's young 'uns and I don't see 'em anywhere around."

"Looks like he was rid hard for a ways," Chance said. "You see the kids anywhere?"

"Nope." It was then it hit me that these tracks we were following were headed right back to the Fitch place. "Chance," I added, "we need to check on Greta and her children real quick like."

I wasn't about to stick around and explain to my brother why I said it. He could figure that out as well as me, so I kicked the sides of my mount and urged him on toward the Fitches'. I rode like the devil getting there, the one thing going through my mind being how decent a family they were and how they didn't deserve to get mixed up in the affairs of our town like they had been. One of the things that had clicked in my mind was what should have been obvious from the start. These yahoos had all but ridden their horses into the ground by the time they left Twin Rifles and were in need of fresh mounts. From the direction they had headed out of town, I should have known earlier that they would be headed for the Fitch spread to get fresh steeds! The thought also briefly crossed my mind that if anything else happened to the Fitch family I didn't think I'd be able to forgive myself.

I was in the lead all the way and didn't even look back to see if anyone was following me, I wanted to get to Greta's that bad. Hell, if it came down to it, I'd go down there and shoot the whole passel of these toughs by myself and leave what was left for my brother to practice on. But when I pulled up just before the rise of their homestead, all of the rest pulled up right beside me. It's reassuring to have friends like that you can count on.

Chance pulled out a Colt and began to check his loads.

"I hope you ain't planning on rushing right down there and trying to shoot your way into the place," I said with a frown.

"And what are you gonna do, just waltz on down and knock on the door?" Chance can be an obstinate sort when he wants.

"As a matter of fact, that might not be a bad idea," Charlie said, speaking up for the first time since we'd left town.

"Are you sure that's a good idea, mister?" Jeremiah Wilson said, a doubting look about him. "There's easier ways of dying than that."

"True, but what if I were to get inside the house and perhaps get their attention while some of you lads snuck up around the back," Charlie offered. He was already dismounting and pulling his jacket off, so all that was visible was the dirty white shirt he wore and the suspenders holding up his trousers. "If I carry this in there with me, I will get shot. Here," he said and handed his pistol to Chance, who tucked it in his waistband.

"Listen, Charlie," I said, "if you do get lucky enough to get in the house without being shot first, there's a good deal of furniture scattered through the living room. You make sure you're quick enough to get behind some when the shooting starts."

Charlie smiled. "I'll remember that." He took a few steps toward the house before stopping to face us, as though talking to us as a group. "Just in case my luck has run out, won't you be so kind as to look after Greta?" Without waiting for a comment or further discussion, he then proceeded over the rise and toward the house, leaving all of us standing there, looking at one another in wonder.

"What in the devil was he talking about?" Emmett asked, pushing his hat back and scratching his head.

"I don't know," I said, just as bewildered as the rest. One thing I did know, and that was that the man heading down toward that house wasn't anything like the man I'd come to know as the drunk of Twin Rifles.

We'd stayed far enough behind the rise so no one would see us yet, and I figured we still had the element of surprise on our side. For one fleeting moment it crossed my mind that if Phineas McDougal and his jailmate were down there, they might recognize Charlie from the jail, although they'd been in different cells. But what if they did? Would the man have a chance? Or had he simply walked into a trap that contained certain death? If I had enough time I would have worried about it, but time was getting to be a commodity we had little of if this plan was to be carried off properly. And the safety of Greta and her children was getting to be more and more important to me with every minute we wasted standing around.

"Tom? Jeremiah?" I said, taking charge of the situation. "Remember that foofaraw we were in out here the other day?" The two brothers nodded silently. "Think you can sneak around the back of that barn like Emmett, Compton, and me did and see if you can flush out any of our friends that might be in there?"

"Consider it done," Tom said and jacked a round into his Henry rifle.

"And boys?" Emmett had a cautious look on his face now.

"Yeah."

"You be real careful of that hayloft topside. These characters seem to think they're might clever." With a wink and a nod he dismissed the two and they were gone.

"Bond, McHale, you grab up your rifles and position yourselves on this rise," Chance said, quickly catching on to what I had in mind. "Those Wilson boys don't flush them birds out the back, they might come flying out the front. You know what needs to be done to 'em?"

"Nail 'em like a Thanksgiving turkey," McHale said in dead earnest. He was pulling his own rifle out of his saddle scabbard.

"Now you've got the idea," Chance said with what I could only describe as a devilish mean smile.

"The three of us are gonna take the ones in the house, is that it?" Emmett said.

"That doesn't bother you, does it?" I said.

"Listen, son," Emmett said, suddenly sporting the same kind of look I'd just seen on my brother, "I don't care how many of 'em there are. You just point in the direction you want me to shoot."

The three of us made our way around the rise, working as quickly as possible toward the rear entrance of the Fitch place. Any minute now Charlie would be approaching the house and trying to talk his way in. I said a silent prayer that he'd make it, for I honestly didn't know what I'd do if these bastards just out and out shot him without letting him in at all. Then we'd really be in a fix.

Halfway toward the back, I got a glance of the corral and saw that the horses there didn't look like the ones that belonged to John Fitch. He'd had upwards of half a dozen, but the ones there now didn't look anything like them. One was a bay that I thought belonged to one of the group of men who'd ridden into town that morning.

"I wonder," I said in a whisper, pointing out the horses in the corral.

"What's that, little brother?" asked Chance in just as low a voice.

"Think those could be the mounts of the fellas we're chasing?"

"You mean they got John's horses and left their own?"

I nodded silently.

"If they're gone, then I wonder who's inside," Emmett said. "Might be we're acting real cautious for nothing." I had the notion he wanted to be where the shooting was and that he'd prefer it be the yahoos we'd tracked out of town that he used as the targets. Not that I could blame him, you understand.

"Hello the house!" I heard Charlie yell out in front of the house. "Anybody home?" All was quiet then as I heard what could only be the front door opening. Then, in a louder than usual voice, I heard Charlie say, "Thank you, sir. Thank you." His voice faded then, but no shots had been fired, so I thought he'd been successful in his mission so far.

"No such luck," Chance said. "Someone's in there with Greta and her children." It was easy to see the prospect didn't make him any too happy, for he liked the family just as much as I did.

"Let's get it done then," I said and led the way back toward the rear entrance of the house. Chance and I had both brought our six-guns, or maybe I should say I'd only brought my LeMat while my brother had not only both his Colt Army Models but the Remington .44 that Charlie had left behind with him. He handed me Charlie's weapon as we neared the back door. Emmett had not only his Colt but my Colt revolving rifle, a weapon he'd taken a fancy to ever since I'd let him use it back at Horse Trap Canyon.

"Nice little place you have here, ma'am," I heard Charlie say once we were at the back door.

"Yes, sir, we like it," Greta said with what sounded like an edge to her voice. It was an edge that I thought contained a growing amount of fear. "Could I get you some more coffee?"

"Why, thank you, ma'am, I really appreciate it." I gave Chance a frown, but all he did was return it, as there was a period of silence next. Then Charlie said, "I really do wish you'd put that cannon away, my good man. I never did get used to having a gun pointed at me."

Chance and I didn't need but to look at one another to know that Charlie had given us the hint we'd been looking for. Someone was in there all right, and they weren't being any too friendly about it.

Too Many Drifters

This was no time to be discussing the situation. No sir. It was a time for doing, and that's just what Chance did. He shoved me aside and got right to the door. Remembering that he'd come through this same back entrance the last time we were here, I didn't make a fuss about it and let him have his way. It's a good thing I did too, for he set about very gently lifting the piece of rawhide that hung out the door so as to ever so quietly open the latch to gain our entry. I hoped he realized that if whoever was inside saw that back door being opened, all they had to do was shoot at the door and the bullets would likely hit my brother.

"Ouch!" I heard someone yell inside at just about the same time that Chance had gained entry. Suddenly there was no more need to be secretive about our activities and I yanked the door open, rushing in and down the back hallway.

The man who had the gun on Charlie was the man who'd beaten up on Joshua and subsequently gotten beaten by the deputy before being thrown in jail with Phineas McDougal. My one glance at the carpetbagger saw him standing off to the side, his hand firmly grasping Greta, a pistol in his hand. I wanted to shoot the sonofabitch then and there, but Charlie had thrown his cup of coffee into the face of the man holding the gun on him. As I ran down the hall, Charlie was rushing the man, knocking him back over the arm of a stuffed chair, upending the man as he did. I don't know if he made the mistake of jumping on the man or if his own weight threw him off balance, but the man never did let go of his pistol even as he fell into the chair. Suddenly Charlie was coming down on the man at the same time the pistol was coming up into his belly. A muffled shot rang out and Charlie jumped in the air some before the surprised look came to his face and he tumbled to the floor.

"Smart ass," I said and shot the killer, twice, once from the LeMat and once from the Remington I now carried. The bullet pierced his chest and I knew he was dead, yet I stood there with my guns pointed in his direction, almost as though daring him to make a move so I could kill him again. I didn't know Charlie that well, but damn it, he was a good man and I was tired of good men being killed.

Chance had run in behind me, stopping dead center in the middle of the room, looking about for someone to shoot. This, after all, was what he did best. But outside of McDougal there didn't seem to be anyone else in the room, other than young Stephen, who was standing behind his mother's skirts, a look of terror about him. When my brother saw that the fat man had grabbed hold of Greta as he tried to pass by him, he simply backed up one step and brought the Colt to bear on the man's thick neck.

"Let go of her or you're dead where you stand, pilgrim," Chance growled, sticking the cold steel of his own pistol into the man's neck. Pistol or not, Chance was calling his bluff.

Phineas McDougal didn't say a damn thing. Either he was too scared or beyond caring, I wasn't sure which. But he didn't move, not worth a whit. Likely he was scared to death.

"You heard him, you filthy bastard!" Emmett yelled from the hallway entrance to the living room. "Let her go!" When the fat man still didn't budge, Emmett stepped forward and, bringing my Colt revolving rifle up in one motion, swung the sharp edge of the butt stock into the side of the man's head. I hadn't heard a deep thudding sound like that since I'd busted up rock with a ballpeen hammer some years ago, but two things I knew. McDougal fell to the floor like a ton of bricks, and if his head wasn't busted wide open it should have been.

"Oh my God!" Greta began sobbing and was soon in Emmett's arms, which made the exsergeant almost as helpless as the man he'd just knocked out. There he stood, a sobbing woman balling on his chest while he put one arm around her to comfort her in as awkward a manner as he likely could and tried to hold on to my Colt rifle with the other hand.

"It'll be all right, ma'am, it'll be all right," Emmett kept repeating to her, although the look on his face was one of a man lost in the desert and not knowing which way to go.

I put my LeMat away and handed the Remington to my brother as I guided Greta toward the couch and had her sit down.

"Round up some water for your mother, Stephen," Chance ordered, still looking the place over for outlaws.

In a short minute Greta's son was at her side, handing his mother a glass of water, no longer the scared young boy I'd seen behind her skirts a few minutes ago. This boy was going to know how to take care of his mother, of that I was certain.

Charlie looked like he was still breathing when I knelt down beside him. "You're supposed to jump over the furniture, not on it, hoss," I said for lack of anything witty to say. "But you done good. We got 'em all."

"Remember what I said." The words bubbled out of his mouth, which was full of blood. "You take—"

"Yeah, I'll take care of Greta."

He smiled then, which was about the same time he died. I could only hope that giving the man my word would ease the pain he was feeling in death.

CHAPTER
★ 20 ★

Emmett was still holding Greta in his arms, still telling her everything was going to be all right, still looking as bewildered as I'd ever seen a cavalry sergeant look, including my brother. I reckon I was as caught up in the moment as Emmett or anyone else there, for I'd purely missed an important fact. Or maybe it was me being as consumed with the death of Charlie, a man I hardly knew but found myself suddenly admiring, as Emmett seemed to be consumed by the hold Greta had on him. It took young Stephen to point it out to us.

"Thanks for helping us out, Chance," the young boy said, tugging on my brother's pant leg.

"Don't mention it, son," Chance said. "It appeared

to me you done a right fine job of protecting your mother just now."

The boy frowned in embarrassment. "No I didn't," he said shamefacedly. "I was scared. I was hiding behind her skirts. Papa said no man should ever do that."

I looked down at the boy, who seemed about to cry, and took him by the shoulders, holding him at arm's length. "Listen, Stephen, I was scared as could be, too. Why, so was Chance and Emmett there. You ask 'em, just ask 'em," I said in as serious a manner as I'd ever spoken to the lad.

"Is that true?" the boy started to say to my brother.

"Damn sure betcha, Stephen," Chance said with a nod and pursed lips. I knew it was hard for him to admit to such a thing, for no grown man likes to admit to being scared, especially with other men around to hear it. Chance would rather eat a cactus whole than admit to being afraid of anything. But he also knew that we were dealing with an eight-year-old boy who shouldn't be feeling shame for his actions. Besides, there was a point to be made here.

"But you guys didn't hide," Stephen said in reply. I reckon that's one thing about discussing things with children: You're more than likely walking into a whole mess of questions you can't rightly answer, at least not properly. Me, I found myself having to do some quick thinking. My brother gave me a second or two longer to come up with something plausible while he spouted off an answer his own self.

"Why, there wasn't time, boy!" Chance said incredulously.

"That's right," I said in quick agreement. "And no place to hide either. Yes sir, that's a fact."

I reckon our answers served to satisfy the boy for the moment, but Chance gave me a look of pure frustration that only confirmed what was going through my mind at the moment: The two of us were having serious thoughts about the future prospect of marriage and the inevitability of having children.

Then Chance gave a quick glance around the room, a frown forming on his face as he said, "Say, where's—"

But Stephen had a quick mind too. "They took Marie," he said, plain and simple.

Chance and I gave one another surprised looks, and I suddenly realized why Greta was still crying. "He's right," she said, pulling her tear-stained face out of Emmett's now soaked shirt front. "They've taken my Marie. They've taken my little girl." No sooner were the words out than she dug her face back down into Emmett's chest, sobbing.

"Sonofabitch," my brother said, almost under his breath. "These heathens ain't good for nothing, are they?"

"Listen, ma'am," Emmett finally said, taking the woman by the arms and holding her back away from him. He seemed to have the kind of understanding in his look now that I didn't recall seeing before. "I know this is right painful for you, but you know you're gonna have to pull yourself together. Besides," he added with a smile, "as much water as you shed, why, you could grow roses in that flower garden out front year round."

"I'm sorry," Greta said, holding back the tears I knew she really needed to get out of her. "I know I—"

"No, no, ma'am." Emmett frowned. "I didn't say I wanted you to apologize. Just don't go fainting on me. These old bones take it hard enough carrying my own body around, and—"

Greta smiled and put a finger to his lips to silence the man. "Thank you for being so kind and understanding, Mr. Emmett."

Emmett doffed his hat and all but bowed for the woman. "My pleasure, ma'am." He coughed nervously, gave Chance and me a glance that dared any kind of smart-alecky remark, then plunked his hat back on his head and pushed it back. Then, in a serious tone, he said, "Now then, what's this about that young lady of yours being took by these killers?"

Chance had made his way to the front door. He opened it and let out a whistle so the Wilson brothers, Bond, and McHale would take notice of him as he waved them on down to the house.

Meanwhile, Greta told us how it all happened. "Stephen came thundering in on his horse, barely making it inside the house before he was followed in by this pack of ruffians led by that man." She stuck her arm out at Phineas McDougal, who still lay unconscious on the floor.

"Ain't no one in that barn," Tom Wilson said, a bit out of breath as he ran into the house, followed closely by his brother, Bond, and McHale. "But I sure heard the fireworks in here." A quick glance at the lifeless bodies of Charlie and the man who had killed him, not to mention the fat man, and he softly added, "Oh."

"I take it Marie and Stephen were out riding?" I asked, remembering how we'd found Nightmare alone a decent distance from the Fitch place.

"Yeah," Stephen said, apparently wanting to take part in the discussion. A forced growl came to his voice, as well as an angry look. "They come up to me and Marie and grabbed her right off of her horse. She said to go get Mama and get help, so I come back here as fast as I could."

"You did the right thing, son," Emmett said.

"No I didn't." Any sense of pride the boy had in telling his part of the story was soon gone, replaced by that same look of shame I'd seen just a few minutes ago. "They all followed me here and Mama almost got hurt."

"Son, you're gonna have to get over these feelings you've got," Emmett said, a frown covering his own face now. "Your mama's depending on you more than ever to help out around here, but ary you're not certain what you're doing is right, why, you'll never be any good hereabouts. Now you listen to me: You done the right thing, here?"

"But—"

"But my aching back! What if you'd rid off into some box canyon and your horse'd thrown you? You'd likely die a slow death and nobody would ever find you! You get in a fix, you head for home. A man's family will always help him out. You bet!" he said with a confident wink to the boy.

"But you don't make mistakes," the boy said. Like I said, these young 'uns have always got a new twist on what you're talking about.

"Mistakes! Me? Why, son, do you know that if I was

to sit down here and now and start telling you how many mistakes I've made in my lifetime, well, do you know that you'd be a full grown man by the time I was through? And likely figure me for a liar to boot!" The words got a smile out of the rest of us, but I doubt that Stephen even saw our reaction, he was that wrapped up in the exsergeant's words. This was turning out to be a day where a lot of grown men were admitting to shortcomings just for the sake of an eight-year-old boy.

"They came in, grabbed a sack full of our food, changed horses, and left," Greta said. "All but these two. I still don't know why they stayed."

"But they took Marie with them?" I asked.

"Yes. Oh, I hate to ask you to do this—"

"We'll get her back, ma'am," Emmett said, as though in charge of the whole expedition. He plucked a pocket watch from his shirt, glanced at it, and added, "Hell, we ain't got much to do for the next five hours of sunlight left in the day."

"I really don't know how to thank all of you."

"Then don't, Greta," Chance said. "People get to stuttering and stammering a lot when that takes place, and I never could stand that kind of hemming and hawing."

"Bond, McHale, I want you to take these two bodies and the fat man there back to Twin Rifles," Emmett said, still the authoritarian. "Truss McDougal up like a Christmas pig and tell that marshal to leave him that way. The rest of us will track down your daughter and these snakes that took her."

"Would you please leave Charlie here?" Greta asked, to my surprise. "I'll take care of him."

Too Many Drifters

"Whatever you like, ma'am," Emmett said with a shrug. He didn't seem to pay any attention to her request, but I found myself wondering about it as we mounted up outside, for it surely did seem a strange one.

It wasn't until we were on the trail again that I realized I hadn't eaten since early morning. But our business seemed important enough to ignore the need for food at the moment. I reckon when someone's life is in jeopardy a body will do that. If the Wilson brothers, Emmett, and Chance didn't say anything about it, I was determined not to either. Especially Chance, food being what it was to him.

Emmett was right when he said we had about five hours of daylight left that day, and we made the most of it. We were entering the hottest part of the afternoon as we took off after them. But instead of five horses there were six we were now tracking. Apparently they had saddled a horse for Marie as they'd plundered Greta of food and whatever had suited them before leaving.

There was only one direction they could ride in to get as far away from the law as they wanted and we all knew what that was when we wheeled our horses and followed them from the Fitch homestead.

South.

To Mexico.

If you remember that Texas was once a part of Mexico, it's easier on your mind as you head south. Some folks figure that once you reach the Rio Grande and cross it, why, the whole area changes into some vicious-looking desert they've been reading about in these penny dreadfuls. Well, you take it from me, those are pure hogwash! I ain't seen the day yet that Mother Nature ever honored a boundary set by any living being. Shoot, half the time the Rio Grande is as dried up as a good share of the land we call desert. And the other half of the time those boundaries are being changed by flash floods and the like. So once we headed south it wasn't that we came on pure undiluted desert, sand and all, as much as the knowledge that gradually, bit by bit, the water holes would be getting farther and farther apart and the land would be getting drier and drier.

It was a shame the horses didn't have more rest than they did, but if we wanted to catch up with the yahoos who had Marie we'd have to do some hard riding. That we did. I'd gauge we covered maybe thirty miles that afternoon, which was probably just what our adversaries did as well. We had one stop for water along the way and only hoped that the Rio Grande we'd be crossing later in the day hadn't dried up this summer. Both our horses and their riders would be awful disappointed if it had.

It was getting close to nightfall when I pulled my mount to a halt and took in the sight before me. I had to blink my eyes twice before I could believe what I was seeing.

"Is that a grove of cottonwoods or am I seeing things?" I asked anyone who cared to answer me.

"Ain't no mirage, that's for damn sure," Emmett said, squinting too.

"What I'm curious about is what's underneath that grove of trees," I heard Chance say as he pulled out his long glasses. He'd made sure and confiscate a pair of glasses that brought the distance right up close to you when you looked through them. The rest of us were silent for a moment as he took a gander. "Well, I'll be damned," he murmured and handed the glasses to me.

"Ain't that the truth," I said as I focused in on what was surely the five men we were chasing and a frightened Marie under the cottonwoods. Why, you'd have thought they were taking their own sweet time getting a fire going and putting on a pot of coffee. "That coffee sure does look inviting," I added after studying their camp for a while.

"It also looks damn stupid," Chance said in reply.

"True," Emmett said. He'd pushed his hat back on his head and had taken to scratching his head as though stumped by what he saw. "Still, it does make a body wonder."

I suddenly found myself wondering if the rest of our group was thinking about the meal we hadn't had as much as I was.

It was Jeremiah Wilson who finally said, "I say leave one man with the horses and the rest of us sneak up on the camp and see if we can surprise those vermin."

"I agree," Tom Wilson said. To Jeremiah he added, "You're elected to watch these nags while we see what kind of meal they're putting on the fire."

"This ain't election day, Tom," my brother growled. "Why don't both of you Wilsons keep an eye on the horses while the rest of us take a gander." For once Chance was acting the role of peacemaker. I knew as well as he did that we didn't need two men watching our mounts, but for the sake of keeping the peace it might be better to have both brothers stay behind. After all, this was no time to be arguing amongst ourselves.

We dismounted, Emmett pulling my Colt revolving rifle from my scabbard as though it were a habit. Chance had his two Colts plus his Spencer rifle. Me, I had my Dance Brothers and had pulled out a spare holster and pistol from my saddlebags. Chance had made the holster himself almost a year ago, and in it I carried my spare six-gun, the LeMat. It would do for the close-in work we were in for.

No one had to tell us to be mighty careful in sneaking up on these birds for we all knew there was no law in this part of the land. If they spotted us and began to shoot, both Chance and me knew that watching out for Marie's welfare was going to take up a lot of our time, which meant making every shot count.

By the time we were in sight of the camp, dusk was just about upon us, but I could see that Marie was sitting on the lap of one of the men we were chasing. I couldn't see whether she was bound or not, but she did appear to have a bandanna wrapped across her mouth. I was about to mention the fact to my brother when Marie made one quick move, grabbing the bandanna and pulling it down off her mouth. Then she looked in our direction—almost right at me, I thought—and let out a scream.

"Chance! It's a trap!"

We couldn't have been but thirty yards from their camp. The man on whose lap Marie had been sitting was a big man, or so it seemed when he stood up and

Marie fell to the ground. Or was she knocked to the ground? I really couldn't tell.

I was about to open fire on them when I heard half a dozen loud clicks to my rear, all of them recognizable as those of long guns. I froze for a moment, the only part of me that moved being my head, as I turned to see a group of Mexicans standing at varying intervals behind us, each shouldering a rifle and pointing it at one of the three of us. Behind them I thought I saw the Wilsons, hands already raised in the air, relieved of their own six-guns.

"Damn," Emmett swore under his breath.

Without so much as a word they relieved us of our weapons. But that was only the beginning of the fun. The big man who had dumped Marie on the ground now grabbed her arm, hauled her half into the air with one good yank, and slapped her hard.

It was a mistake.

You grow up in this land learning to respect womanhood. Only a coward or the lowest of life forms ever hit a woman. It simply wasn't done. And those who did deserved to be horsewhipped. Well, Chance had killing this man on his mind and set out to do just that, taking giant steps toward him and not really caring if the Mexicans behind us shot at us or not. Big Fella just stood there over Marie as she cried for him not to do it anymore, a leer on his face if ever I've seen one. No one else moved or said a thing, although I wasn't sure whether it was because they were afraid of Big Fella or because they wanted to see what my brother would do.

"Coward!" Chance yelled out when he was only two

steps away from Big Fella. It got the man's attention all right, which was just what Chance wanted. When he turned to see who'd spoken to him, Chance hit him hard in the face twice, knocking him backward the first time and drawing blood from the big heathen's nose the second time.

I'd followed Chance in and would have yelled out a warning but it would have been too late. Before I could get the words out, one of the henchmen in this outfit cracked the barrel of a rifle across Chance's head, sending my brother to the ground like so much dead weight. No sooner did he fall than Marie, who I'd suspected had a crush on Chance for some time now, was kneeling by his side trying to take care of him, although she had nothing to take care of him with.

I was about to rush to his side my own self when I felt the cold hard steel of one of the rifles behind me sticking in my neck.

I froze still, knowing that at this moment I was much more afraid than I had been when I'd charged in through Greta's back door this afternoon.

From the camp I heard a man yell, "See, friend, I can set a trap too."

CHAPTER
★ 21 ★

They had us pretty well tied up by the time they got around to throwing some water in Chance's face. Not much, you understand, just enough to bring him around. A cupful was all they'd spare.

"What the hell—" my brother started to say, shaking his head before realizing how much pain that rifle barrel had put him in. "Ouch."

"Ain't so tough now, are you?" Big Fella growled at Chance, a leer of satisfaction passing across his face that only men like that are capable of having. It made you want to kill him right then and there if you had the weaponry. But then these characters only act like that when they have the upper hand, which is just what they had at the moment.

I reckon Chance knew they had the upper hand too, but even in his pain he could give just as good as he could get and did his own form of growling right back at Big Fella, especially when he gave a sideward glance and saw the bruise on Marie's face. Greta's girl was sitting on Chance's right, her back up against the same cottonwood Chance was leaning against.

"Turn me loose and I'll show you how much of a man you never was," my brother said with a snarl. One thing about my brother, he's got what we call staying power. I didn't have to listen to any stories of his exploits in the Union army during that war to know such a fact. I'd experienced it on more than one occasion before the War Between the States even started. I reckon Pa brought us up to be that way. At first, in my youth, it had all seemed like a lot of hero stuff, but I'd found out as the years went by that it was a necessity more than anything on this frontier. Only the strong survived and if you weren't capable of that, well, you faced an early grave.

"She's all right, Chance," I said, second guessing my brother's next question. "Roughed up a mite, but holding her own, I'd say." I saw the forlorn look on Marie's face and remembered how sad her brother had been earlier that afternoon and added, "One thing's for sure: Ain't no doubt she's John Fitch's girl." I looked right at her as I said the words, tacking on a rather proud smile after I finished. It did the trick and the young lady, roughed up though she may have been, was soon blushing with the kind of pride she should have been feeling.

"I'll say," Emmett said, catching on to my train of

thought. "You're a right resourceful young woman, if I do say so."

"Shut up, all of you!" Big Fella said with another grumble that was meant to scare. The only effect it had was on Marie, who soon lost the smile she'd briefly sported.

"Don't you worry, honey, I'm gonna kill the flannelmouth before this is all over," Chance said in a hard, even tone, "and he ain't never gonna bother you again. I guarantee it." No one had to ask whether my brother was serious about what might be construed as an idle threat. Men like Chance don't make idle threats. Fair warning, maybe, but never idle threats. But it sure did put a burr under the saddle of old Big Fella, who promptly laid the flat of his hand alongside my brother's face, the sound of which you could hear for some ways off, I gauged.

"Shut up, I said!" he yelled once more.

"You stop that, you big bully!" Marie said, her bravado showing. No doubt about it, she was John Fitch's daughter all right.

"You shut up too, or I'll show you what a good beating is really like." Big Fella sure was brave spouting off to people already tied up. The more he kept doing it, the more I became convinced that he was a coward, just like my brother had originally labeled him.

I wanted to ask them what they had in mind, what they were going to do with us now that they had us captive, but I had a sickening feeling in the back of my mind that I already knew. When they were taking their own sweet time eating the evening meal about an hour later, I happened to catch part of their conversation, which only confirmed my own dark thoughts.

"I tell you, Logan, we gotta get rid of 'em," Big Fella's deep voice was saying. "And the sooner the better. Hell, they ain't nothing but extra weight, and you know as well as I do that we can't afford that right now."

"Yeah," one of the others agreed. "Being on the run means traveling light. They'd only get in the way."

"What do you want to do?" the one named Logan said next. "Kill 'em off?"

"I reckon it's the quickest way," Big Fella said.

"May I offer a suggestion, señor?" a Mexican who spoke English surprisingly well said, suddenly taking part in the discussion. I'd almost completely forgotten about the Mexicans now in camp. I noticed that they'd gathered in their own little group off to the side of the campfire—four of them in all, if I was correct in my count.

"Speak your piece," Big Fella said. I could tell from the tone of his voice that he didn't really care for the Mexicans that much, had likely taken them on simply to get the drop on us when we came to his camp, as he knew we would. In fact, I had no doubt in my mind that when the four Mexicans were through, Big Fella and his men would shoot them in the back in a second.

"Life is too short to waste in a land such as this," the Mexican said. "Especially for someone like the señorita," he added, nodding toward Marie. "I have no use for the other men you have captured, but I do know of men who would make good use of the girl. I could easily take care of her for you rather than let her die."

A look of pure terror came over Marie's face now as she heard the conversation about her. I could tell she had an idea of what this man had in mind. The men this Mexican was talking about were more than likely Comancheros or bandits of sorts, which would scare the daylights out of any Texas woman. The Comancheros had anything but a reputation for being decent human beings. *Nasty* and *evil* were better words to describe the disposition of any one of them. And when it came to women, they were known only to use them as sexual objects, brutalize them, and then kill them, unless they traded them off to the Comanche Indians in the area, a fate also feared by any white woman. So the terror Marie was feeling was well justified, I was sure.

"You got any American money you can pay for the girl?" Big Fella asked. He must have known what would happen to Marie as well as any of the rest of us. The kind of reputation held by the Comancheros is not one to be held in check; it is heard of and known by nearly everyone.

The Mexican shrugged. "Perhaps fifty dollars of your American money between the lot of us."

"No," Big Fella said, shaking his head, "it ain't enough. Try digging out a hundred and fifty. More, if you've got it."

The Mexican was quickly back in conference with his three compadres, the bunch of them hashing over the subject before growling what I thought to be a few cuss words. They made one collective glance at the girl and then Big Fella before digging into their pockets and spreading what they could find on the ground before them. Finally they shrugged and turned it all over to the man who had done the original talking for them. He, in turn, faced Big Fella.

"One hundred dollars in your American paper money and gold coin, amigo," the man said in a simple, forthright manner and tossed the money on the ground in front of him. "That is all we have between us, my friend. As you gringos like to say, you can take it or leave it."

I'd bet a dollar these Mexican fellows could get upwards of five hundred dollars for a young girl like Marie about to enter womanhood, and they likely knew it better than Big Fella and his crew. Big Fella, on the other hand, was in no bargaining position but likely looking to turn a fast dollar. Being on the run does that to you, I reckon.

"You've got a deal," he said. I thought I saw a gleam in his eyes as he got up and made a move for the money now strewn on the ground across the camp.

"Not yet, amigo," the Mexican said with a grin, scooping it all up before Big Fella could reach him. "There is nowhere to go this late at night. We will wait until tomorrow morning to make the exchange. Besides, we are tired. It has been a long day and I desire my rest." He must have seen the greed in Big Fella's eyes, for he added, again with a knowing smile, "Please do not do anything foolish, amigo. You must know that we sleep light and shoot straight." You had to be a fool not to know what he was getting at, especially when his three traveling companions each took a tug at their pistols and gave Big Fella and his bunch that same evil smile.

"Yeah, sure," Big Fella grumbled with a frown. With that, the trade seemed to be finalized and the two sides sat back and rested for the night.

"You hear that?" I whispered to Emmett, seated on another side of the tree they'd plunked me down at.

"Yeah. Don't look too promising, does it?"

"Not by a long shot. Any ideas?"

"Not at the moment, but we've got all night to figure it out," he said.

One of the Mexicans, who identified himself as Pedro, took it upon himself to draw from the pot of beans on the fire and began to feed us one by one. You have to remember that our hands were tied behind our backs and our feet were bound as well, so other than shifting your ass around a bit, it was hard to do much moving. I didn't know why he did it and I wasn't about to ask.

"That's mighty kind of you, friend," I said when he got to me and began shoveling beans into my mouth. I even managed to get a few sips of his water. It crossed my mind while he was feeding me that it might be worth trying to cultivate some kind of friendship here, but I discarded it, figuring these fellows were just as bad as the ones we'd been chasing. Still, there had to be a way of getting out of this fix. I just hadn't thought of it yet.

It wasn't a night for sleeping, that was for sure, but after an hour or two of wracking my brain I still hadn't come up with a way to free ourselves. The only possibility I could think of was Marie scooting over and sitting back to back against Chance and trying to undo his ropes, but it would be too noticeable. Besides, Marie had fallen asleep, and trying to waken her would only get the guard's attention, maybe even the whole camp's.

I don't know what time it was when I faded off to sleep. I don't even know if I was the last one to do so. What I do know is that I fell into a dreamlike sleep that had me going in and out of confrontations with Pa. I reckon that deep down I loved him like a son is supposed to love his father, but I also knew that there were days that he really got on my nerves, especially of late with those smart-alecky comments he'd been making to me whenever he walked on the scene. Take that fight Pardee Taylor had gotten into with Emmett outside Ernie Johnson's saloon. There I was, standing there just taking it all in, when Pa had walked up and said, "I can't keep getting you out of these scrapes, son." Why, that was embarrassing as all hell! Someday I was going to have to talk to him about it.

"I can't keep getting you out of these scrapes, son." There it was; he'd said it again.

"Pa," I was saying to him, getting ready to chew him out something fierce, when suddenly I couldn't say what I wanted to say to him. But then dreams are kind of strange, if you know what I mean.

"I don't know what I'm gonna do with you," Pa was saying again, speaking a mite softer this time. It was then I felt a pressure being applied to my jaw as my head began to shake back and forth uncontrollably. Suddenly I discovered I wasn't dreaming anymore. I opened my eyes, realizing that the night air had cooled off quite a bit and that I was feeling cold. I was also well aware of where we were and what a fix we were in. But before I could get a handle on the rest of it, my head was jerked to the side, and my eyes opened wide at what I saw.

It was Pa!

"Got yourself in another difficulty," he whispered, shaking his head at me in a frown. "Sshh." I don't think I was ever so glad to see him, but I passed my comments over, instead silently leaning forward so he could cut the bonds tying my wrists. Across the camp, where the guard was once sitting, I saw only the slumped-over body of the man. Behind him, hidden behind another cottonwood, was Joshua. Pa's deputy had either hit the man on the head or dug a thumb deep inside the man's collarbone, causing the man to fall into total unconsciousness. So far as I knew, the Mexicans didn't have a guard posted at all.

Pa was cutting Emmett's bonds when Chance spoiled the whole thing. "Give me that pistol in your waistband, Pa," he said out loud. Pa took one last swipe at the ropes between Emmett's feet, then dug into his waistband and grabbed and tossed a Remington to my brother.

Like the reckless fool he can sometimes be, Chance stepped out in the open, ready to take on all comers. But I knew as well as he did that he had someone special in mind. Big Fella was reaching for his own six-gun as he came out of whatever sleep he was in—a reflex action for this type of man, I reckon. The thing is he never cleared leather. Chance had been walking as he'd cocked his own gun and shot the man between the eyes. Marie would never have to worry about this sonofabitch hitting her again.

Then Chance spun around as another shot went off. It came from the Mexican who'd done the bartering with Big Fella earlier in the evening. He was right: He must have been a light sleeper, and he was fast with a gun. But he was a shade off my brother if what he'd intended was a head shot. His bullet had grazed Chance's skull, spun him around and knocked him down all right, but it hadn't killed him.

He never got the chance. Pa had tossed me his second gun, and I shot the Mexican dead where he lay, only half up in a crouching position.

Suddenly the whole camp was awake and you'd have thought it was the Fourth of July the way the fireworks were going off. But from the direction and frequency of the lead flying through the air, I had the notion we were getting more gunfire from the Mexicans in camp than from the yahoos we'd originally followed here. I reckon most of the rest of us had the same feeling too, for Emmett, Pa, Joshua, and me were shooting in that general direction for all of ten or fifteen seconds. Mind you, it felt more like ten or fifteen minutes. It was all the time we needed, for in that time frame, well, the other three were just as dead as their compadre was.

I didn't pay attention to the scream when I first heard it, being more concerned with getting shot at long enough to stay alive to find out what it was, I reckon. The gunfire hadn't all subsided yet, for the outlaws we'd tracked here had rolled out of their bedrolls too, shooting as they withdrew from camp, it looked like. It was when I turned my attention to them that I recognized the scream as coming from Marie.

They'd taken her!

Too Many Drifters

The bonds of her feet had been cut but not her hands. She had been forced to mount a horse at gunpoint, and now she was being led out of camp with the man I recognized as the one called Logan, along with one other man. Emmett had grabbed someone's knife and had just finished cutting the Wilsons loose by the time he noticed Marie and the two men riding off from camp.

I could barely make out their figures as they rode away, suddenly becoming aware that the faint light in the east was an indication that sunrise wouldn't be far off. We had apparently slept a good deal of the night before Pa arrived to help us out.

Pa was leaning over Chance, who was now regaining consciousness. "Easy now, son," he said when Chance tried to get to his feet, only to fall back to the ground. "That's a nasty piece of work they done on you. Better take it easy for a bit."

"What about—"

"The one they called Logan and another got away with Marie," I said in what must have been a less than joyous tone.

The fire was back in Chance and he tried once more to gain his footing. It was a shaky proposition, to be sure, but he made it. He had that killing look about him when he was on his feet, but he wound up leaning against Pa when he tried taking a step or two.

"You best take it easy, hoss," Emmett advised. To Pa, he said, "Marshal, if you can take care of things on this end, me and Wash will play catch-up with the two that got away."

"Are you sure?" Pa asked, knowing that we could easily get more volunteers to ride along with us; all we had to do was ask. "Seems to me they're managing to stay one jump ahead of you boys."

"Well, I won't deny that's a fact, Marshal," Emmett said, "but I can guarantee you it's gonna come to a right quick halt before the day's out."

"You can believe it, Pa," I threw in for good measure. "And Pa?"

"Yeah, son."

"You won't have to worry about getting me out of this fix, for that ain't gonna happen again."

"I believe you, Wash, I believe you."

CHAPTER
★ 22 ★

Pa made quick work of explaining how it was he and Joshua had shown up to rescue us while I gathered up my six-guns and holster. It seemed that Bond and McHale had gotten Phineas McDougal back to the Twin Rifles hoosegow that same afternoon we'd left to track the five riders south. The two had also done an adequate job of explaining how they'd captured McDougal and came to have him in their possession. Pa had figured that I'd gotten myself into another one of those fixes he was always talking about of late and had made Bond and McHale special deputies for him, ordering them to stay in the jail and make sure that Phineas McDougal didn't escape this time. It was then that he and Joshua had saddled up and rode hell for leather in the direction Bond and McHale had indicated, riding hard even after dark to get to the outlaw camp. It was an hour before sunup that they'd made their move and snuck into camp, cutting loose as many of us as possible before anyone in the camp was awakened.

"You sure you're gonna be able to catch up with them bastards?" Chance said in a voice that was anything but foggy. It was the first time he'd spoken up since getting creased by that Mexican's bullet, and you might have expected that he'd be confused in his thinking. But not Chance. Like I said, when the man has a mission on his mind, why, there ain't nothing that stops him.

"Betcherass I'm gonna catch 'em," was my firm reply. I can be a determined sort at times too, especially when someone's life is in danger and that someone is a nice young lady like Marie.

"I reckon this is what you had in mind, huh?" Tom Wilson said, leading old Nightmare over to me. He'd unsaddled my own mount and placed it on the mustang I knew was as fleet as any I'd ever ridden.

"That's it," I said and gently patted the horse's muzzle, trying to make friends with it the way I'd seen Emmett do with those wild ones we'd broken not a week before.

"Now you've got the idea," Emmett said and patted the big horse's neck. Old Nightmare was going to have a lot of friends real quick if this kept up. Of course, I also suspicioned that this steed knew what it was he was going to be called on to do too, and that was put his very heart into catching up with Logan and his friend and saving Marie from anymore dire straights she might fall into. For a moment it sounded like some of that slop I'd read in one of those silly dime novels, but this situation was as real as they get.

"Are you sure just the two of you will be enough to catch them, son?" Pa asked.

"Bet on it, Pa," I said. With a smile, I added, "One Ranger for one riot, remember?"

"Sure," Pa said, returning the smile. Pa knew as well as I did the story about a small town that had been thrown into civil revolt and, fearing the bad element would take over, had sent for help from the Texas Rangers. Not long afterward, a man rode into town, sporting the badge of a Ranger. When asked why there weren't more Rangers with him to quell the riot, the lawman replied with a shrug, "You've only got one riot." The Ranger had indeed taken care of the riotous situation and his story had spread. Nearly all of us who had been Rangers at one time or another knew of it. Seeing Pa smile like that told me he understood what I had in mind.

I grabbed my reins and mounted old Nightmare, turning the mustang toward the trail Logan and his riding partner had left. Emmett swung into his own saddle and put his heels to his horse in order to catch up with me.

The sun was coming up over the eastern horizon as we left camp. Me, I was getting hungry as well, but suddenly it didn't matter how long I'd gone since I'd last been fed. Getting Marie safely back from those outlaws was all that was important to me now. Hell, it was the only thing going through my mind now. Eating could wait.

It was hard telling exactly where these yahoos were

headed, although it seemed that off and on they were using the same trail we'd followed when they'd fled south once they left the Fitch place. It was getting toward midday when we stopped the horses for a rest at a water hole.

"Looks like they're heading back to the Fitch place," Emmett said, a worried look about him. It was the first time I'd seen the man show that much concern about anything since arriving in Twin Rifles.

"You sure your mama ain't staying with Greta and her children?" I asked as I watered my horse and eased the cinch on him, letting him blow.

"What?" At first he had a confused expression on his face, but it soon had a good deal of red creeping into it too. It didn't take long for the man to get the drift of my implication. "Well . . . she is a good-looking woman."

"I'll give her that, all right." No doubt about it, Greta Fitch was a beautiful woman, one that just about any man could fall in love with. "Of course, I'd keep in mind that she's just lost her man," I added with a note of caution. I also made sure I was more than arm's length away from Emmett when I said those words. Men like Emmett, I'd learned, could get real picky about what was said to them and how it was said. I reckon Chance was as good an example of that as anyone I'd seen of late.

"Oh, hell, Wash, I ain't been doing nothing but daydreaming about the woman, that's all," he replied in an offhand way. "You know as well as I do that I couldn't give her nothing to live for. Nothing like the man she was married to, anyway. Why, I've gone from soldiering to drifting as a career and likely won't change much in the near future." He paused a moment in thought, before looking at me and adding, "I wouldn't worry about me making a fool out of myself with that lady. It just ain't meant to be."

While Emmett was talking, I reached inside my saddlebags and dug out a portion of what had once been a loaf of bread Greta had baked for her family. It had apparently been part of the food these outlaws had ransacked from her home before riding south the day before. Me, I'd grabbed this portion while Pa was doing his explaining of how he'd come to our rescue. Like I said, my stomach was giving off the rumblings of hunger even back then. I handed a piece to Emmett.

"It ain't much," I said, "but at least it'll keep those yahoos from hearing our bellies growling before they hear the rest of us coming."

"Was that what I been hearing all morning?" Emmett said with a smile, relieved, it seemed, to be talking of something else.

"Likely," I said around a mouthful of food. I sipped real easy on my canteen of water, reminding myself that we'd do well to fill the canteens before leaving the water hole.

Nothing else was said about Emmett and what he felt for Greta Fitch that afternoon, but I sure did find myself wondering about just how real a possibility that might be for either of them. Why, if you looked at it in a realistic way, there wasn't a man who'd come west who had much more than the clothes on his back or in his saddlebag at the start. And if he was carrying a small treasure in gold, it was likely the gold his watch was made of rather than any coin of the realm he could spend. Everyone knew that a woman was more than worth her weight in gold in this land. Anyone could learn how to cook or sew, but it took someone special to help a man raise a family or even make a family, if you get my drift. And as far as I knew, a woman was what was needed to fit the bill when it came to making and raising babies. So even if you started out with nothing, a man and a woman usually wound up making something out of it.

I reckon if you thought about it, why, it was a good deal like the country we lived in. America had all started as one big idea, one big dream. But we were unlike any other country that had ever been born. We had no basic religion, no conquered land mass to live upon then. Most of all we didn't have a history to pull our roots from. Instead, we'd all come from every which place on this earth a body could think of, been thrown into one big pot to stew for a while, and finally come up with what they called "American" as a way of life. Hell, we'd made our own history as we lived it. I reckon that was part of what had inspired John Fitch to be an American so much. So if a nation could find its way, couldn't the people who made up that nation do the same? It was something to think on.

We took one last drink of cool water, refilled our canteens, and were soon on our way again, tracking down Logan and his friend. We rode at a steady pace for a while before I pulled my horse to a halt.

"What is it, Wash?" Emmett asked, pulling the reins on his own mount.

"I don't think you'll have to worry about Logan heading for the Fitch place," I said.

"Oh?"

I dismounted and searched the ground before me,

making certain my eyes weren't playing tricks on me in the afternoon heat. It wouldn't be the first time a mistake had been made during the hottest part of the day for man and beast. I checked the hoofprint and nodded back at my riding companion.

"He threw a shoe," I said.

"That'll slow 'em down some," Emmett agreed. "But what makes you think they won't head for the Fitch place? As I recall, they left their original mounts there, didn't they?"

That had been my line of thought too. After a day or two, those nags these yahoos had been riding would still be a better bet for riding than the worn-out broncs they were on now. "True, but you're forgetting where it was we first saw these buzzards."

"Oh yeah, your box canyon," Emmett said with a nod, remembering now.

"Yup. Horse Trap Canyon. And unless I miss my guess, they'll be turning west shortly," I said. "Right now that canyon is a lot closer to horses than the Fitch place would be to these birds." Even in the short time they were camped there, it would have been hard to miss the amount of horses in that box canyon. The fact that it was a box canyon would make these pilgrims think it would be that much easier to rope and saddle another horse. I had to smile to myself as I tried to picture Logan and his friend trying to deal with that bunch of wild mustangs. It would be a real chore for them.

"I see what you mean."

I was right. Maybe a quarter mile on, their trail took a turn to the west, heading for the canyon Chance and I had called our own, basically because we'd chased those wild mustangs into it and managed to keep them there. By twos and threes we cut them out, drove them back to our ranch, and set to breaking them on an individual basis.

We made a brief stop at the turn in the trail, but only long enough for me to pull my Colt revolving rifle from its scabbard and hand it to Emmett before he could pull it away from me. He'd grown as attached to the weapon as I had, although he'd become much more proficient in using it in methods other than shooting. I began to wonder if having it in his possession didn't bring out the animal in the man.

Our gain on them was steady from there on out that afternoon, and it was close to late in the day when we caught up with them. Or maybe I should say it was about that time that we had Horse Trap Canyon in our sights. Both Emmett and me knew that we'd have better cover when it was closer to dusk, our shadows being harder to make out as we moved in on the canyon entrance. But we also knew that we'd be taking a chance on hitting Marie once darkness had fallen upon us.

"I say the sooner we get 'em the better," Emmett said once we'd come to a halt. It was as though our minds were both thinking the same way.

"Do it on foot from here on in?" I asked.

"No use making yourself a bigger target than you already are." Emmett nodded and we both dismounted. "I'll do the long shooting," he added, holding up the Colt rifle, as though to indicate what he'd be doing it with. "Once we get there, I reckon it's your show. I'll back you up."

"Never mind that," I said, checking the loads of my

Dance Brothers and LeMat pistols. "If you see something that looks like a clean shot, kill him."

We moved in on the mouth of the canyon from opposite sides. Me, I was hoping neither of these two birds was able to climb the walls of that box canyon any better than Chance or I had been able to do. For the most part, the walls were sheer rock inside with hardly a spot big enough to get a foothold. The few spots we had discovered that were climbable only went halfway up the face of the wall. With that in mind, I tried to bolster my courage with the certain knowledge that neither Logan nor his partner could shoot at us from anywhere high on the canyon walls. Still, in the back of my mind was the even more certain knowledge that it only took one well-placed shot to kill a man. I reckon that was why I felt like I'd pulled the palms of my hands out of a bucket of water as I made my way toward the canyon.

They didn't shoot at us until we were a hundred yards away from the canyon mouth, and that came from what I gauged to be ground level. One shot I recognized as coming from my Colt rifle and Emmett's direction made them tuck their heads back inside for cover as I did some fancy running before another shot could be fired my way. It wasn't until I dove for the ground that I realized that my own six-guns were useless at this range, which made me little more than a sitting duck. What I needed was to get closer so my guns would have some effect. Besides, I had no reloads for either of my guns. I reckon it was part of Pa's belief that if you couldn't do it with one shot you didn't deserve anymore.

When Emmett fired a second shot I did some more

running toward the outer wall of the canyon, in the background hearing the spent bullet ricochet a couple of times inside the canyon entrance. If it had been possible I would have cussed the exsergeant something fierce for doing that kind of shooting. You'd think he'd forgotten that Marie was inside those walls too. Still, the shot had done the job and I managed to make it to the outer wall, sweat pouring down the middle of my back as I flattened it against the hard rock. I could only assume that Emmett had made his destination too as I made my way closer to the opening of the canyon.

The wooden gate Chance and I had constructed had been opened and was now only half closed. For one lone instant a terrifying thought crossed my mind: What if these birds had let those wild mustangs loose? Chance would be killing mad if that happened! Hell, we'd put a lot of work into capturing those beasts in the first place. Having to go out and do it again wouldn't set well with my brother. Hell, it didn't set well with me! But no horses had come out since we'd arrived here, so maybe they were still in the box canyon. On the other hand, I didn't hear the sound of any horses inside either.

Emmett had worked his way to the other side of the mouth by the time I was near the entrance. I couldn't see anyone across the way on his side of the canyon and simply shook my head when he looked my way. He did the same when he'd taken a gander at my side of the entrance. Neither of us had to be told that Logan and his friend had pulled back inside the canyon.

"Ready?" Emmett said aloud.

Too Many Drifters

I shrugged. "Ready as I'll ever be."

"Then what are you waiting for?" he said and took three quick steps around the corner and entered the canyon. Me, I did the same thing, each of us with our guns at the ready.

I reckon I'd gotten so concerned about Marie, who I still hadn't heard a sound from, and keeping her alive that I'd forgotten about what awaited us inside. I'd forgotten about the tiny plateau Chance and I had discovered about halfway down the right side of the canyon. It was one of those levels we'd found enough footholds to climb to, maybe twenty-five feet off the ground. If you were a romantic sort, I reckon it would be a nice place to spread a picnic lunch with your woman for an afternoon, for it held a good view of the area as well as a bit of privacy once you moved back out of sight. But it was killing that was in the air today, not romance, and it was from that small plateau that I heard the shot fired. Of course, the bullet hit me in the shoulder before I heard it. That's always how it is. By the time I knew where it had come from I had been thrown back against the sharp rock of the entrance, feeling pain on my left side, both front and back.

But I wasn't the only one who'd heard it. Emmett was damn near as good with guns as he was with his horses. In the same instant I was thrown back against the wall of the canyon, Emmett stepped out in the open, spotted the man who'd ambushed me, and shot him through the heart. I only got a brief glimpse of him as he fell off the plateau to his death and saw that it wasn't Logan. It must have been his partner. Emmett stood there in the open, almost as though daring someone to take a shot at him. Me, I still had my guns in my fists. Pain or no pain, I did my best to stay alert, for this dance had only begun.

"I don't know who he was," I said, my eyes now darting every which way for the likes of Logan, "but the devil oughtta be making a place for him in hell about now."

"I reckon that's one lesson the bastard won't forget," was all Emmett said, holding his Colt rifle at the ready, squinting even in the afternoon sun.

"Chance!" I heard Marie yell in a voice filled with terror. Then I saw her, jumping out of a crevice in the wall to our right. I'd explored it before and knew that it was wide enough for maybe a couple of men to work their way into but not a horse. I only saw her for a second, waving at me, likely thinking her hero, my brother, had come to her rescue. Then Logan stepped out and hit her with a hard right cross, knocking the girl out as she crumbled into one small lump on the floor of the canyon.

"Sonofabitch," I growled and took a step forward, halting when Emmett stepped out in front of me and fired a round from the Colt. The bullet ricocheted back and forth a couple of times as Logan ducked back inside like some scared turtle trying to protect himself with his shell. But whether he knew it or not, Logan had backed himself into a corner there was only one way out of, and that was through us.

I felt like I had a piece of that rock stuck in the back of my shoulder but knew it was the bullet that had pierced me that was making me feel so miserable. I wanted to lay down and sleep, maybe next to Marie to try and comfort her. But she was laying there out in the open and if Logan got as piss-ugly mean as Big

Fella had, why, he might just take to shooting the little girl. I couldn't let that happen, I just couldn't. Greta would never forgive me.

I don't know how I did it, but I ran to the wall that opened up the crevice. I must have put one foot in front of the other, for at the time it seemed like the only way to get it done. You can bet I remember slamming into that wall, especially with my wounded shoulder and all. Hell yes, I remember it.

Emmett stayed where he was, doing his best I thought to cover me as I worked my way closer to the crevice. I reckon he knew we had to take care of both Logan and Marie, although in different ways, if you get my drift. But you know, hoss, even in all that pain, I found myself feeling a certain camaraderie with the man, maybe because we were both working toward the same goal and didn't have to discuss it. We just knew. We were working together the way a good team should, the way we all had back during the war. I reckon that was one of the feelings you came away from the war with, no matter which side you fought on. Everyone worked together toward one common goal. Sometimes you made it and sometimes you didn't. But Emmett and me, we were by God gonna make it!

I moved toward the crevice, stopping when I was maybe eight feet away from the opening. Then I waited for Logan and wasn't disappointed. He was as fidgety as we were, I reckon, and was sticking his arm out and shooting his pistol at Emmett in only a minute. Emmett fired back and Logan stepped inside the crevice again. It was what I needed, what I wanted him to do.

I took one step away from the wall, then used both guns to shoot against the opposite wall of the crevice. I fired maybe six shots all told, but they had their effect, did what I wanted. I'd fired at different levels, hoping the ricochets would hit Logan where I thought he was standing. They did, for I thought in the roar of gunfire I heard the man moan.

I'd gotten his attention and maybe he was hurting as much and as bad as I was now. Served the bastard right!

He hadn't fired on Marie, who still lay unconscious on the ground, but I knew what a man as desperate as Logan must now be likely to try. I couldn't wait any longer. I had to take care of him now, even if it meant my own death. All I could think of was how Greta would never forgive me.

My legs felt like they had nothing but lead in them as I took three or four big steps until I was right out in the open, right in front of the position I thought I'd find Logan at.

But he wasn't there!

A shot rang out from down the crevice where the man had slowly moved back. My shots must have made him as delirious as I had felt at times since being hit, for his shots went wild, except for one that took my hat off my head. He'd moved about six more feet inside the crevice and I could barely see him there in the darkness. By the time my eyes picked him out, he was cocking his pistol again, but he wasn't shooting at me. He was shooting at Marie!

I couldn't see where the bullets hit. All I knew was that two of them went off and past me before I stepped inside and emptied my LeMat into the man, watching him bleed like a stuck pig as he slid down the side of the crevice wall, dead.

Emmett was at Marie's side by the time I turned around, taking her in his arms like the daughter he'd never had.

"Is she hit?" I asked, afraid of what the answer would be.

"No, she's fine, just fine, Wash," Emmett said, slowly sweeping loose hair from the girl's eyes, then running his rough hand down her soft cheek. He smiled when she came to, and to my surprise she smiled back at him. "You're gonna be fine, sweetie, just fine."

Emmett led both Marie and me out of the canyon, sitting us both down and tending to us as best he could. Her jaw hurt like hell, but all he could do for me was stifle the flow of blood from my shoulder and do a sneaky job of pouring homemade whiskey on the wound. My scream would have woke the dead.

Inside half an hour he had the bodies of the dead men on their horses and me and Marie on ours. Then we set out for the Fitch place, hoping we'd make it there before sunset.

I don't know how long it took but we didn't make it there until that night. It was dark, the kind of dusk that settles on a place for the first hour or so after the sun sets. I must have slept all the way, for I'd no sooner been pushed up in the saddle than we were at the Fitch place, Greta standing there crying.

"The issue was never in doubt, ma'am," I heard Emmett say. "You best give a good deal of the thanks to Wash, here, for he's responsible for getting us out of that fix."

Finally, someone was giving me credit for getting us out of a fix instead of in one! I looked at Greta and did my best to smile, although the pain was overcoming me.

"Yes, ma'am," I said, then fell off my horse.

It was a good thing Emmett was there to catch me, for I was ready to hit the ground and didn't really care one way or another. The fact of the matter is, I passed out then.

CHAPTER
★ 23 ★

From what they told me the next morning, Greta worked some kind of miracle getting that slug out of me that night, ably assisted by Marie throughout the whole operation. Then, after maybe four hours of sleep, she was up at dawn again and cooking one hellacious breakfast for the hungry under her roof. She was quite a woman, no doubt about it. She was also quite a cook, for it was the smell of coffee and ham that brought me out of what must have been a deep sleep.

I looked around and got my bearings, discovering that I was laying on Greta's big living-room couch. When it came to me what had gone on the previous day and how I'd gotten here, I asked, "I didn't get blood all over this thing, did I?"

"By God, I told you he was too mean to die!" Emmett said with what sounded like a good deal of gusto. He set down his coffee cup and pushed himself back from the kitchen table and a plate now only half filled with ham, eggs, and spuds. A big smile came to his face as he wandered over my way and stuck out a big paw. "Welcome back to the world, son." Then, yanking a thumb over his shoulder at Greta, he added, "The woman here, why, she wasn't certain you'd make it or not. Do you know she'd make one hell of a surgeon if we could get her to enlist in the army?"

"Oh shut up, you big fool," Greta said as she pushed her way past Emmett and leaned down and kissed me full on the lips. I've got to tell you that her doing that purely shocked me, although it was likely for the better than the worse.

"Whoa, ma'am," was all I could think to say. "You keep that up and I won't need any other medicine to get well quick."

But her tone had turned somber now, as she said, "I want to thank you for saving Marie's life. I don't know how to repay you, Wash. I just don't." As soon as she got the words out, she had a corner of the apron to her face, dabbing at her eyes as she softly cried in an unashamed fashion. I'd like to think they were tears of happiness, but I imagine she still had a good deal of grief to handle over John's death as well.

"Don't you worry none, Miss Greta," Emmett said, placing a big hand on her shoulders. "You save the life of a man as good as old Wash here, why, I'd say you squared all the accounts for some time to come, ma'am."

"That's a fact, Greta," I added, suddenly realizing that I was talking to the woman who saved my life. "You don't owe me nothing." There was a lot of silence for a minute or two before I added, "But I sure do like the smell of whatever it is you're fixing for breakfast, ma'am. If Emmett will give me a hand to my feet, why, I do believe I can make it to your table ary you'd serve me up a portion."

"Of course," she said and was soon back at the stove.

After I was in a sitting position, Marie helped me to my feet. "I'll make sure you don't fall over," she said, but by the way she was holding on to me, I had the feeling it was one big hug from a grateful young lady more than any other kind of support she might be giving. I don't mind telling you I appreciated it too, as much as my arm was hurting.

But Marie didn't stop at helping me to the table. She stood right there and all but waited on me hand and foot, pouring me coffee and cutting my meat for me since I was only good with one hand for the time being. I don't think I've ever seen a prouder smile on the girl either. I just hoped she could keep it that way the rest of her life.

After the meal was over, Greta made comment about the horses of the men who'd ransacked her place, wondering what she should do with them. I explained that if she was willing to part with them, Chance and I could likely sell them to the army and turn the money over to her. It seemed like the decent thing to do for a woman who had lost her husband and was now all alone in the world, with no one to fend for her. She consented and I kept the subject in mind as something to talk to my brother about.

"Well, ma'am, I reckon I'll be taking my leave," Emmett said shortly. "I originally hired on to bust some broncs for the Carston brothers and I reckon I oughtta get back to it."

"As long as you're willing to take your time riding into town, I'll ride along with you, Emmett," I said, surprising all of them, I reckon.

"Then the children and I will ride along with you," Greta said. "I must do some shopping anyway."

The ride to town was a silent one, most of us going over our own thoughts, I reckon. I would have headed for the ranch were it not for delivering the bodies of Logan and his friend to Pa. I reckon there was also a certain satisfaction I wanted to have in making sure Phineas McDougal saw what had happened to his cohorts. To me that man simply hadn't been scared bad enough and it was something he needed badly.

I sometimes wonder how much of a hand Fate plays in the things we do. Was it chance, perhaps, that had Pardee Taylor walking out of the general store at the same time Greta was pulling her buckboard up to it? I don't know. But what followed was one of the strangest encounters I'd ever seen.

"Good morning, ma'am," Pardee said in the most civil tone I'd ever heard him speak in. "Let me help you down." He then held his hand out to assist Greta in getting out of the buckboard.

"My my, Mr. Taylor," Greta said in a voice suddenly stiff with formality. "Acting the part of a gentleman, and sober as well?"

Pardee blushed, embarrassed more for himself than anything else, I thought. "Yes, ma'am. Look, I'm real sorry about your husband dying and all. I really am."

Greta raised a curious but stiff eyebrow. "Really? I thought you were the one who wanted John to go back to where he came from."

I thought I'd seen redder color from a cut steer, the way Pardee was blushing, but not much. "No, ma'am, I was wrong. He had as much right to be here as anyone, I reckon."

"I have heard that it is divine to forgive," Greta said. "Just so you don't have to live any worse a life than I have, Mr. Taylor, I forgive you."

"Thank you, ma'am," Pardee said in a humble voice. "Thank you kindly."

When he didn't move, Emmett said, "If you're waiting for her to bless you, son, you're in the wrong church. Now scat."

Pardee walked off, noticeably relieved now that he'd gotten it off his chest. Watching him go, I thought I'd seen a miracle of sorts.

"Wash, you'd best get to the doctor and get that wound looked at," Emmett said. "Don't you worry about these characters," he added, nodding toward Logan and his friend who were draped over their horses. "They ain't going no place. I'll get 'em over to your daddy's." To Greta he tipped his hat and said, "It's been a pleasure knowing you, ma'am."

We all went our separate ways for about an hour or so. The doctor checked me for infection and put some salve on the wound before rebandaging it, assuring me that I'd be all right in a week or two, as long as I didn't do an awful lot of strenuous work. Chance wasn't going to like that when it came time to bust some more of those broncs.

I was headed for Pa's office, wanting to get caught up on the news of the aftermath of Phineas McDougal's capture, and was just outside the office when I heard a gunshot inside. Without a second thought I was inside the office, my Dance Brothers six-gun cocked and in hand, looking for someone to shoot.

I needn't have. There stood Greta, a pistol in her hand, gunsmoke curling up toward the ceiling. Halfway out the cell door was Phineas McDougal, lying flat on his face, a small pool of blood spreading from beneath him. Stranger than this sight was that of Emmett, kneeling next to McDougal, doing something with the keys to the cells and the fat man's hands.

"He was one man I couldn't forgive," she said in a voice that had no tone at all to it, which was strange considering the hateful look on Greta's face. She was in some kind of shock and I didn't want to get shot my own self, so I holstered my Dance Brothers and slowly pried the six-gun from her hands.

"What happened?" Pa said, rushing in, a gun in his fist.

"Looks like a prisoner got shot escaping jail," was all I said.

CHAPTER
★ 24 ★

I knew it was coldblooded murder, what Greta had done to Phineas McDougal. Hell, I think we all knew that. But there wasn't a jury in the state that would convict the woman when presented with the facts of the matter. Some folks deserve to die more than others, and McDougal, he deserved it more than anyone that day. I reckon that was why Pa didn't go too far into the matter in the way of investigating it. As for Emmett squatting down there next to the dead man, I figured that he was simply trying to help the woman out of a tight spot by making it look like Phineas McDougal had again somehow gotten hold of the keys to the cell and was trying to escape.

Whatever the true story might have been, it was the

end of a carpetbagger and his efforts to bilk the people of Twin Rifles out of their money. Once word got around what happened to the man and his gang, why, you could pretty well be certain his kind wouldn't show up in our town for some time to come.

I reckon the only thing that really bothered me about the whole affair was the death of Charlie and how Greta had insisted on keeping him there at her place. A week or so later I wandered out to her place to see how she and the children were doing and happened to notice that John and Charlie were buried side by side. In town a few days later, I asked Pa about it, figuring that he knew most of what went on hereabouts anyway. He did.

"Did John ever tell you a story about how he'd run into some big-time gambler way back when and won his wife in the process?" he said.

"Yeah," I replied. "He didn't say it outright but I figured it was him he was talking about."

"Well, I don't want you spreading it around, son, but from what I was able to gather from John, old Charlie, our town drunk, was Greta's first husband," Pa said in a secretive voice.

"You mean old Charlie was the one he got into that card game with?"

"Sure was. Odd thing was they met up just before coming here and got to liking one another. I reckon that was why John would buy Charlie a drink when he came to town."

It explained a lot and I let it be, just as Pa had suggested.

Bond and McHale and Emmett stayed on and helped us break the rest of the wild mustangs we had. I even managed to take on Pardee Taylor as a rider about a week after everything had quieted down. He turned out to be a fairly respectable man if you gave him a chance. My brother and I did.

Three months later we were done and had to let them all go, for the rounding up of more horses to chase into Horse Trap Canyon was something Chance and I could do by ourselves.

It didn't surprise me that Emmett showed up at Greta's one morning and told her she needed a good man to run the place. She agreed and he found himself a job taking care of what was largely a farm.

Ever since he'd been back from our mission, Emmett had talked about Greta and I knew he had a bad case of that woman. The next time I saw him was at the big shindig in town. Emmett hadn't been a sergeant in the cavalry for nothing, and, being the bold-talking man that he was, one day about six months after John Fitch had died, he walked into Greta's kitchen and flat out told her she needed a man in her life.

Like I said, that was when I saw Emmett next, at the big shindig in town. It was when Emmett and Greta got married.

FROM POCKET BOOKS AND BOOK CREATIONS, INC. COMES AN EXCITING NEW WESTERN SERIES

ABILENE
BY JUSTIN LADD

- ☐ BOOK 1: THE PEACEMAKER .... 64897/$2.95
- ☐ BOOK 2: THE SHARPSHOOTER .... 64898/$2.95
- ☐ BOOK 3: THE PURSUERS .... 64899/$2.95
- ☐ BOOK 4: THE NIGHT RIDERS .... 64900/$2.95
- ☐ BOOK 5: THE HALF-BREED .... 66990/$2.95
- ☐ BOOK 6: THE HANGMAN .... 66991/$2.95
- ☐ BOOK 7: THE PRIZEFIGHTER .... 66992/$2.95
- ☐ BOOK 8: THE WHISKEY RUNNERS .... 66993/$2.95
- ☐ BOOK 9: THE TRACKER .... 68151/$2.95
- ☐ BOOK 10: THE GENERAL .... 68152/$2.95
- ☐ BOOK 11: THE HELLION .... 68153/$2.95
- ☐ BOOK 12: THE CATTLE BARON .... 68154/$2.95
- ☐ BOOK 13: THE PISTOLEER .... 69312/$2.95
- ☐ BOOK 14: THE LAWMAN .... 69313/$2.95
- ☐ BOOK 15: THE BARLOW BRIDES .... 69314/$2.95
- ☐ BOOK 16: THE DEPUTY .... 69315/$3.50

Simon & Schuster Mail Order Dept. AJL
200 Old Tappan Rd., Old Tappan, N.J. 07675

POCKET BOOKS

Please send me the books I have checked above. I am enclosing $_____ (please add 75¢ to cover postage and handling for each order. Please add appropriate local sales tax). Send check or money order—no cash or C.O.D.'s please. Allow up to six weeks for delivery. For purchases over $10.00 you may use VISA. card number, expiration date and customer signature must be included.

Name _____

Address _____

City _____ State/Zip _____

VISA Card No. _____ Exp. Date _____

Signature _____ 292-15